THE
Culper Ring
NOVELLAS

THE

Culper Ring

NOVELLAS

ROSEANNA M. WHITE

WhiteFire
PUBLISHING

THE CULPER RING NOVELLAS
Copyright © 2020 by Roseanna M. White

FAIRCHILD'S LADY
Copyright © 2013 by Roseanna M. White

A HERO'S PROMISE
Copyright © 2014 by Roseanna M. White

ISBN: 978-1-941720-42-4

WhiteFire Publishing
13607 Bedford Rd NE
Cumberland, MD 21502

Fairchild's Lady

Prologue

Versailles, France
April 1789

A mask provided no anonymity. Not for her. Remi would know her by her eyes if she let him look into them, know her and hold her close to his side all evening. The way he did at every other dinner, every other ball.

But not tonight. The desperation she felt inside had been growing so long, and now it nearly choked her. She would escape, *must* escape, if only for an hour. Keep her eyes down and *live* behind layers of powder, feathers, and silks. Live, for once, behind the mask.

She glanced up only long enough to assure herself that Remi was on the other side of the room, engaged in a conversation with Grandpère. Then she spun the opposite way—directly into a solid chest. *"Pardonnez-moi."*

Hands gripped her shoulders to steady her, warm and large, and a chuckle brought her gaze up. *"Bien sûr*, mademoiselle."

The baritone voice sent a strange trill along her nerves. Pleasant…mostly. Her brow furrowed as her mind flitted through all the men she knew at Versailles, all the nobles she had met over the years. She tried in vain to light upon who stood so tall. Had shoulders so broad, a chin so strong. A smile so charming, with eyes such a lively brown behind his mask.

Coming up blank, all she could do was smile in response. "I am sorry. I was not watching where I was going."

"I shall forgive it." He released her shoulders and bowed as the orchestra struck up a new song. "For the price of a dance?"

Caution made her want to glance over her shoulder again, but she refused. She would take this one dance, this one ineffectual grasp at freedom. "*Oui.*"

The music she had heard a thousand times before. The dance she had performed too often to count. But these past years, only with Remi. Remi, with his possessive gaze. Remi, with his dangerous smile. Remi, with his crushing whispers. Demanding what she could not, *would* not give. Not until the shackles were firmly around her wrists.

"You say '*oui*,' mademoiselle, yet your mind does not seem to be following your feet to the dance floor."

That equaled a victory for Remi, too, did it not? That her every move, every *thought* must revolve around him. She squared her shoulders, lifted her chin, and gave the stranger her most charming smile. "I am here, monsieur."

Again his chuckle thrummed over her. He lifted her hand and pressed a kiss to her knuckles.

Never before had her knees gone weak at such a move as they did now. Her fingers felt so warm in his, so…safe.

As if safety were ever anything but an illusion. Like freedom.

The stranger's eyes sparkled. "I hope you are. The evening

suddenly looked so much brighter with the light of your gaze upon it."

Flattery and charm—no strangers to anyone at Versailles. Yet the way he said it…she drew in a deep breath and let herself think, if only for a heartbeat, that he meant it.

He led her through the minuet, his every motion fluid grace. Every female gaze, it seemed, was upon him. But despite the beguiling grin that remained on his lips, his eyes were frank. Without deceit. Confident, seeking, inviting.

Was it possible?

For the first time in three years, she dared to want. A conversation, nothing more. A conversation with a man who didn't try to devour her with every sweep of his gaze. And so, when the set ended and the tall stranger led her off the dance floor and cocked his head toward a door, she made no objection.

She left. Without a glance over her shoulder, without acknowledging that frisson of fear that clawed its way up her spine. She left. Left Mére, left Grandpère.

Left Remi.

The feeling of safety next to the stranger was surely deception, the desire to tuck herself to his side pure madness. But with the moonlight shimmering its silver magic down upon the gardens, she couldn't help but think that a sip of insanity might be exactly what she needed most.

Perhaps it would be enough to see her through the bleak forever before her.

One

7 July 1789

Revolution. Oh, how Isaac Fairchild hated that word. He reigned in his mount and drew in a long breath, his gaze taking in the palace before him that he had hoped never to see again. Versailles stretched long and dazzling in the sunshine, its gardens as resplendent as ever, its edifices as grand.

Its grandiosity but an ill-fitting mask over a country on the brink of uprising. Because it was too stark a contrast to the peasants starving mere miles away.

Blood would be shed in France—soon, if that sizzle of warning through his veins were any indication. And for the life of him, he couldn't remember why he'd agreed to put himself in its path. He'd had enough of revolution, enough of intrigue to last him a lifetime. He had been hard pressed to accept the task of gathering information for England three months ago. Why in the world had he volunteered to come back after making his escape?

A horse cantered up the road in his direction. Fully prepared to give way and paste the expected lack of emotion onto his face, he instead smiled when he recognized the haughty posture of the rider and the ridiculous plume on the hat. "Jean-Paul!"

His old friend grinned as he circled his horse around to face Versailles. "*Bonjour,* monsieur. And how is our charming comte d'Ushant today?"

Fairchild's smile went uneven. After knowing all his life he would never inherit his father's earldom, being called by the French equivalent never ceased to feel strange. But Jean-Paul could hardly greet him by name, and the real comte d'Ushant was in no position to mind that Fairchild was borrowing his identity once more. "*Bon. Et vous?*"

Jean-Paul shrugged and flipped the feather back over his hat from where it had fluttered before his face. "I did not expect you back so soon, *mon ami.* When I received your message…"

"*Oui,* I know. I did not expect it either, but this business is of a personal nature." Unbidden, the face of the Earl of Poole flashed through Fairchild's mind. Those sorrowful eyes, pleading with him to save his wife and daughter, so long lost to France. To bring them back to England before revolution swallowed them.

Fairchild had tried arguing that an absence of twenty-five years surely had deeper roots than he could hope to overcome in one short visit, but the earl had begged him, had called on Fairchild's connections to his two sons—the elder, with whom he had attended school, and the younger, who had sent him here those months ago.

'Twas pity that had moved him, though, to try to find the

missing Countess of Poole and Lady Julienne Gates. Pity for the father's fathomless eyes.

"Personal, eh?" Jean-Paul smirked.

"Hmm." Fairchild shifted in his saddle and tried to keep his mind from conjuring up another set of fathomless eyes. Tried but failed. Just as he had for the last three months. Every time he blinked, it seemed, he saw those ice-blue irises, so striking behind their mask that he had scarcely noticed anything else about the young woman at the masquerade. At first.

Then would come the memories of her smile. Her laugh. The dance they had shared, the stolen promenade through one of the gardens at Versailles. The uncounted hours they had spent talking in that night of moonlight that had since seemed removed from this reality, of a world unto itself.

He didn't even know her name. He had asked, but she had laughed and declared the mystery to be the whole point of a masquerade.

His fingers contracted around the reins and then relaxed again at his command. He knew enough of the court of King Louis XVI to understand that more often than not, that "mystery" was to allow for infidelity and trysts. And more than once he had wondered if the young lady who filled his mind so fully was someone else's wife.

Father above, please, let it not be so. And if it is, please remove her from her from my thoughts, from my heart.

He shook himself and focused on Jean-Paul. On the task at hand, which was the earl's wife and daughter, not a pretty French aristocrat he would likely never see again, save for in the dreams that had plagued him these months. "I must seek out the daughter of the marquis de Valence. Do you know him?"

Jean-Paul sniffed in that way only a Frenchman could.

Nothing but a small motion, hardly a sound, yet it conveyed more meaning than Fairchild could hope to interpret. "I know *of* him, of course, as everyone does, but being an untitled noble myself, I have never moved in his *échelon*, shall we say. Nor have I met his daughter or granddaughter, though I have seen them at court. Beautiful women, both. *Très, très belle.*" Jean-Paul arched a brow. "Which is it you have an interest in, mother or daughter?"

"Neither and both." Seeing no need to volunteer more, Fairchild offered only a smile and nudged his horse into a trot. "You know the ladies to see them, then? You could point them out to me? If I could bypass the marquis altogether, that would be preferable." More expedient, he hoped.

Please, Father God. How often had he prayed this same thing on the journey to France? *Please let Lady Poole and Lady Julienne hear me out. Let them be swayed. Help me remove them from harm's way.*

Jean-Paul inclined his head. "I know not where their residence is, but if we happen across them, then *oui*. The marquis will no doubt be embroiled in the meetings of the états-*general.*"

A chill swept up Fairchild's back despite the warm summer sun. "They convened it, then." Proof that the news he had brought back to England with him three months ago was accurate. France was in dire straits, out of money and out of options.

A snort matched the look of wariness in his friend's eyes. "*Oui*, they convened it. And the commoners declared themselves a National Assembly. There is rumor that they intend to remain assembled until they have drafted a constitution."

Fairchild opened his mouth to reply, but nothing came

out. Not when he caught site of the field of soldiers drilling. Nay, then his throat went altogether dry. He had seen such formations often enough, though usually the men he regarded bore the scarlet jackets of his own regiment. "Why so many soldiers?"

Jean-Paul chuckled. "The king may have given in to the demands of the Third Estate, but he is no fool. The military has been arriving both here and in Paris, I am told."

Though the masses of enemy soldiers inspired another drumroll of nerves, Fairchild drew in a deep breath and sent heavenward a deep prayer. He realized the mustering might actually be a blessing. With so much turmoil surrounding the court, no one would pay any heed to him. No one would pause to wonder why he sought out a certain madame and her daughter.

And indeed, no one looked twice at him as he followed Jean-Paul to the massive stable complex. He grinned at the same boy who had taken care of his mount upon his last visit, tossed him a coin, and followed his friend back out.

"*Un moment.*" With his gaze fastened on a few gaily clad young ladies in the distance, Jean-Paul hastened away. Fairchild leaned against the building and watched the young man weave his charm. Bowing, fawning over ivory hands, speaking words Fairchild had no hope of hearing from here—and which he suspected would only make him fight a roll of the eye were he nearer.

One of the ladies huffed and lifted her chin, but Jean-Paul only grinned and motioned toward Fairchild. Whatever he said seemed to appease the girl, for she smiled and made reply. A few moments later Jean-Paul strode his way again, satisfaction gleaming in his eye.

"Come, *mon ami*. To the *Grotte des Bains d'Apollon*. They say your ladies made mention of heading that way this morning."

Nay. Fairchild pushed off the wall, careful to keep his features calm. Surely the young ladies were mistaken. Of all the acres of gardens, of all the acres of palace, why, *why* would the countess and her daughter be in the grotto? The very one he had wandered to that night while the masquerade reeled on inside? The very one where his ice-eyed lady had strolled with him, her fingers woven through his?

Jean-Paul turned toward the nearest garden path. With little choice but to follow, Fairchild drew in a long breath. *She is Yours, Father in heaven. You know her name, as I never will. You love her as I can only imagine doing. She is Yours. And so I give her, again, to You. Help me put her from my mind. Help me focus, instead, on the earl's family. Help me to find them, dear Lord above.*

The paths through the gardens were a veritable maze of crisscrosses and odd angles, making him grateful for the guide. It had been quite by accident he had ended up at the legendary statue of Apollo and the nymphs three months ago, and he doubted he would have been able to find his way there again without a few wrong turns.

At last the grotto came into view, its stones carefully placed to look natural and chaotic. They formed a cave where the main statue resided, as if it were the very one in which Apollo took his repose after bringing the sun into the sky. To the sides stood the lesser sculptures of his horses being tended, and before it stretched a small pond with grasses and flowers to give it a primordial look. All within the protective shield of an English-style thicket.

Fairchild's fingers flexed, as if expecting to find smaller ones held within them. Rather than the rustle of the grasses, his ears strained to hear that of ice-blue silk.

He shook it off and sent his gaze around the grotto, seeking flesh-and-blood ladies instead of the apparition of memory. There, on a bench amid the trees, he found two. He nodded their direction. "It is they?"

Jean-Paul squinted and tilted his chin up. Then he bobbed his head, sending his plume waving. "I believe so, *oui*. Though I cannot introduce you, as I am not acquainted with them."

"No need to worry, *mon ami*. I will handle this part on my own."

"In that case, I will seek you out later. In fact, I will go now to be sure they assign you the same apartment you had last time." That was why he and Jean-Paul got on so well—the Frenchman knew when to smile and take his leave.

Their entrance into the vicinity hadn't disturbed the ladies a bit. No doubt they were well accustomed to the passing by of other nobles out for a promenade, which suited Fairchild fine. He took a moment to study them, to try to discover by mere observation if they could be the women he sought.

The mother would be the right age. Though her hair was more gray than brown, what color he saw matched the auburn Lord Poole had instructed him to look for. He edged closer, though careful to remain behind the shield of a flowering bush. Yes, her eyes were green. She was seated, so he couldn't be sure of her height, but his guess was that her stature matched the description as well.

And the daughter—her profile was all he could see, but that was encouraging. The same nose that both the Gates brothers had, with its gentle slope. The same set to the eyes, hair with the same golden glint as the elder son, though this

young lady's seemed to borrow a bit of her mother's red-brown
as well. Lovely, to be sure, also as he expected, given the well-
acclaimed looks of the rest of her family.

A bird flitted overhead warbling a tune, and the young lady
turned her eyes to follow it.

Eyes of an icy, glacier blue.

Two

Julienne watched the golden plover wing its way out of sight. Far better that distraction than the conversation she wished she could keep from having. Again.

"Julienne, heed my words. It is crucial you follow my direction, or the duc may yet lose interest."

Would that he would. Julienne tried to summon a smile—a difficult task, with the memory of last night's encounter with the duc still so fresh in her mind. "Mère, please…I cannot. It is disrespectful and…and wrong to be making such plans. He is yet married."

Her mother waved that away. "His wife will pass away within the month. It is a sad reality, *ma fille*, but reality nonetheless. And a duc must be looking toward the future of his line. When this terrible disease takes his wife, he must move quickly for a new one, one who can give him heirs."

Julienne turned her face toward the grotto's grass-edged pond. The trees gave them a semblance of privacy, but solitude was never complete at Versailles. And so her face must always be free of any emotion she didn't want to hear as the next topic of gossip.

Free of the yearning. Free of the guilt. Free of the fear.

But inside, her thoughts raged. Three years now she had put her life on hold to await the duc's proposal—a proposal that couldn't come until his sickly wife succumbed to the disease eating her away.

Three years to bear the guilt of claiming a connection to a man not free to seek one.

Three years to feel his gaze slide over her, to parry his advances, to refuse his ever-increasing whispers that no one would expect anything else but that they taste now what they would enjoy fully once wed.

Three years to come to hate him. And hate herself for being the means by which a man abandoned his wife, and in the time when the duchesse needed him most.

"Mère, I..." She drew in a long breath and lowered her voice to a bare murmur. "He does not love me. It is only an attraction, and I am hardly in my first blush of youth anymore. He will not want me once my looks fade. When my waist thickens with that heir he so needs. He will seek another then, a young mistress, and I cannot...I cannot bear it. I *will* not bear it."

Mère's soft touch bade her look at her again, and Julienne found her eyes to be, as always, full of love. "My darling girl, you know I want only the best for you. And I would not urge you this direction did I not believe it to be best. The duc is unmatched in all of France. He can offer you security, happiness, and affection. You underestimate his feelings for you, *ma chérie*. He loves you."

Did he? No, Julienne thought not. She had acquaintance

with enough men to know the difference between lust and love. To know when interest was only in the facade so carefully crafted and when it went deeper.

She had learned through pain and tears how to tell. Though until three months ago, she had thought them *all* interested only in the facade.

Mais non, she couldn't think about that night, the stranger. He was more dangerous than any aristocrat with an eye for seduction. Still, she could hardly sit in the grotto and escape thought of him.

Her eyes slid closed. And with the darkness came the image of stars twinkling above that midnight stroll. The sensation of a large, strong form beside her, leading her onward with a gentle surety she had never experienced before. The feel of her fingers caught in his. The sound of his laughter.

But memories of his laughter always led to his voice.

"*Pardonnez-moi*, mesdames."

Her heart seized. Julienne's eyes flew open, though she focused her gaze on her hands. Why look up, after all? It wouldn't be him. It never was. How many times had she let herself imagine over the last months that he had sought her out, had found her? *Mais non*. She always looked up to find someone too short, too round, too thin, too broad, too narrow, too *something*. And then she would realize the voice wasn't quite so deep a baritone, didn't have quite the right timbre.

Didn't have that accent that had made dread snap her lips shut when he asked for her name.

Yet she had dreamed of him all these months. Ah, what a fool she was.

Mère stiffened on the bench beside her. "*Bonjour*, monsieur. Can I assist you?"

Julienne snuck a glance just in time to see the intruder bow. He, as most other fashionable men these days, was dressed *à l'Anglais*, in simple breeches that molded to muscular legs, an unadorned waistcoat, a well-tailored but unembroidered coat. He had doffed his hat, revealing hair of a warm brown, bound at the nape.

Something tickled the back of her neck. *L'espoir.* Which proved her a fool yet again. Why should she hope? There was nothing left to hope for—she was trapped in this web life had woven for her. Promised to a man she didn't want, who couldn't claim her yet was too influential to be refused.

Non. No hope rested in the stranger who had surely not been what he seemed anyway.

A stranger who had been just as tall as the man before her proved to be upon straightening. With shoulders just as broad. A chin just as strong, though little else had been visible beneath his mask. This man, though, had a face clearly discernible and handsome enough to warrant the way her heart sped. He certainly carried himself as a noble, with confidence and poise in every line.

So had the man from the masquerade. But his voice, his accent…

Julienne clasped her hands together, the pressure of fingers upon fingers the only way to school her wayward thoughts. She would *not* dwell on the stranger—not that one nor this. Even if the first had spoken to her very soul on their walk, and if the one before them now tempted her to flutter her fan and play the coquette just to earn a smile.

She was too old for such nonsense.

But he smiled despite her lack of fan fluttering, and dimples winked out on either side of his mouth that made her glad she sat, for surely they would have turned her knees to melted wax.

The man placed his cocked hat back upon his head. "*Merci,* madame. I have need of nothing and only stopped because of how familiar you look. You must be the daughter of the marquis de Valence, *n'est-ce pas?*"

That quickly, Mère went from stiff and cold to warm and friendly, ushering him nearer with a wave of her hand. "*Oui,* I am the comtesse de Rouen. You know my father?"

The man inclined his head and smiled again, those dimples wreaking havoc on Julienne's heart as he came a few steps closer. "Does anyone at Versailles *not* know him? Though I confess I am at my château more often than at court."

"And you are?"

He bowed again, though not so deep this time. "Charles Mercier, the comte d'Ushant."

Julienne kept her brow from creasing, but only barely. There, as he said his name...that accent. So very slight—her mother certainly didn't seem to notice it, given the way she preened and held out a hand—but it was there. Just as it had been that night.

Was it possible? Was this man, the comte d'Ushant, the man from the masquerade? The very question made her pulse redouble and her palms go damp. It couldn't be. It was her imagination again, surely. A bit of rebellious, unreasonable hope. Nothing more.

She'd nearly convinced herself when he looked over and caught her eye. Then she nearly choked on the air she had just drawn in.

Mère cleared her throat. "Have you met my daughter,

Julienne? The two of you seem as though you are trying to place each other."

He extended his hand, and her fingers moved of their own volition toward his, though higher reason said she ought to withhold them. But before she could command her mutinous limb back to her side, her fingers settled on his palm. Warmth washed over her, just as it had done that night. That unexplainable yearning to wrap her arms around him and beg him to take her away from here filled her.

Ridiculous.

His dimples made no appearance now as he held her gaze. "I believe we shared a dance at a masquerade some months ago, *non*? I did not learn your name at the time, of course, but I remember your eyes."

A dance. Simple words, yet she read so much more in his own eyes. Didn't she?

"Ah." Mère smiled even as she settled her gaze upon their still-touching hands, reminding Julienne that she ought to have pulled her fingers away already. Yet cold swept up her spine when she obeyed the silent command. "My Julienne is indeed unforgettable. The duc tells me so regularly."

Julienne swallowed against the acrid taste in her mouth, but it would not go away. As she watched, the light in d'Ushant's eyes dimmed, as though a lamp were being trimmed. "Your husband?"

Julienne raised her chin. "No. I am not married."

"He is her fiancé," Mère said, not so quickly that it would sound pointed, but not so slowly as to allow even a moment of hope.

Hope again—such a foreign thing to be coming up so often.

Julienne wanted to argue the point about her betrothal, but she dared not. Instead, she prayed that as he studied her face, he would see it wasn't so simple. That she wasn't so despicable as to wander in a garden with one man while betrothed to another.

Yet she was. For surely a woman despicable enough to let a man court her while still married could easily cross that other line, could she not?

Take me away, Father in heaven. Show me how to escape from this guilt.

The comte nodded at her mother's pronouncement and retreated a step. From his stoic countenance she couldn't determine anything of his thoughts. He smiled, but it failed to light his eyes again. "The duc is blessed indeed to have won the hand of so fetching a mademoiselle. And doubly blessed to be gaining such a lovely mother."

There, again, that *je ne sais quoi* in his speech. What was it that felt odd? The timbre? Perhaps it was nothing—a result of being more often in Ushant than at Versailles. A regional difference. Perhaps…

Mère laughed, her posture relaxing a bit. "You are a charmer, monsieur. I cannot understand why you say you are not often at court. You would surely be a favorite."

Ah, *oui*. One dimpled grin and surely all Julienne's friends would fall over themselves for his attention. Her stomach went tight as she imagined Marie and Georgette fluttering lashes and fans his way. Not that she had any right or reason to begrudge them his regard. He was not for her. She dared not encourage any other man, and besides…this one, she had already decided, hid something. And until she could determine what, wisdom dictated she stay far from him.

Wisdom did not always make the most beguiling companion.

The comte chuckled and looked around the grotto. Was he imagining it in moonlight? Picturing himself on this very bench beside her? "I confess I prefer the quiet of country life. Though I am quite fond of this particular niche in the gardens."

Again it was a struggle to draw in a breath.

Her mother hummed a bit as she looked around. "I never cared overmuch for it, though it has of late become Julienne's favorite spot as well."

His gaze arrowed into her again, and she felt heat creep up her neck and into her cheeks. The smile he gave her was lopsided. "Has it?"

"Something we have in common, monsieur." Her lips tugged up even as her mind spun, recalling all the other things they had discovered they had in common that night. Their opinions on Mozart's *Don Giovanni*, on the writings of Rousseau and Montesquieu and Pascal. Their thoughts on the fledgling United States, on faith. On everything.

Mère stood and urged Julienne up too with a hand under her elbow. "We will let you enjoy it. It was a pleasure to make your acquaintance, monsieur, but please excuse us. We have an engagement pending with the duc."

"Certainly. Thank you for taking the time to speak with me." He bowed again.

Julienne couldn't have explained, had anyone asked, why she so wanted to pull away from her mother. Why she wanted to reach out so she might brush his hand as they walked past. She mustn't—she didn't. But she wanted to. And the moment they swept past him, the sun seemed to dim.

Her mother's fingers tightened on her arm. No doubt once they were out of hearing, a lecture would be forthcoming. Yet another hushed reminder that they could not possibly cross the duc.

"Oh, madame?"

Mère halted. They were nearer him now than when they had been seated, only a step beyond him. Close enough to reach out and touch. Though her mother pasted on a smile, Julienne still felt her impatience in the fingers on her arm. "*Oui?*"

The comte's smile had gone cool. Almost....hard. Some might even call it calculating. "I bring you greetings from your husband."

Julienne would have dismissed the statement as confusion on his part had her mother not gone deathly pale. "Pardon? You must have mistaken me for someone else after all, monsieur. Le comte de Rouen has long been deceased."

He positioned his hat back on his head. "Yes," he said—in English. *English! That* was the accent! "But the Earl of Poole is still quite well."

Whatever in the world? "Mère?"

"Hush, Julienne." Her mother's fingers dug even deeper into Julienne's arm, and her voice was low as a secret. Her gaze hadn't left the comte's face. "I cannot think what you mean, young man." Yet her words, too, were in English.

His eyes softened again, though they barely flicked to Julienne before focusing on her mother. "We both know you do, Lady Poole. Please, hear me out. Your husband wants to see you. And his daughter."

For a long moment, the words seemed to hover outside Julienne. They made no sense, and not only because they were in a tongue she rarely used at Versailles. How could her mother possibly have married someone else before her père? Who was this other daughter?

Then his meaning hit, and a gasp slipped out before she could restrain it. Never had her father been anything but a specter in their family, a once-man who was rarely spoken of and then without affection. But never had she considered that he might not *be* her father.

Her mother squared her shoulders. "We really must be going." Her words were again in French, and at a normal volume. "But my daughter and I were planning a ride through the country in the morning, just after breakfast. Perhaps you would be so good as to escort us, monsieur?"

He tilted his head. "I would be honored."

"Tomorrow, then." Mère let go of Julienne's arm and spun around again.

Julienne remained rooted to her spot, her gaze fixed on the handsome face only a step away. Questions wanted to riot, but they settled when his eyes locked on hers. Nearly every night she had dreamed of those eyes, as warm a brown as a cup of *café*. They were trustworthy eyes. No matter the questions, no matter the unexplained, that much she knew. Whoever this man really was, she could trust him. *Did* trust him.

Somehow her fingers laced with his. She didn't realize she had lifted her hand, but there it was, halfway between them. She shifted so that if Mère turned around, Julienne's body would block her view.

His fingers tightened around hers, his thumb stroked over her knuckles.

"Come, *ma cherie*." Impatience colored her mother's voice.

Both squeezed, both let go. Julienne sighed even as he grinned at her and said, "*A demain*, Julienne."

She nodded and memorized his face so that her dreams could recall it without flaw that night. "Until tomorrow."

Her mother linked their arms together, no doubt to propel her more quickly away. All too soon they had left the grotto behind them, though Julienne couldn't resist turning her head as they were about to round a corner. Yes, he was still there, watching them go.

"Foolish girl." Mère pulled her onward, worry now making her voice heavy and low. "Please remove that look of longing from your face. You cannot know...if the duc realizes..."

Julienne lifted a brow, though even as argument sprang to her tongue, she took note of the lines around Mère's mouth and eyes, deepened just in the last minute. "If he realizes what, Maman? That I find another man handsome, or that I am apparently not the daughter of the comte de Rouen?"

Though she had spoken at a bare murmur, for a moment she thought her mother would clap a hand over her mouth, so frantic were the eyes she turned on her. "Hush, child! Well you know that the hedges at Versailles have ears, just as surely as the walls and rooms."

"We are safer out here than anywhere. Tell me, please. What did he mean? Who is the Earl of Poole?"

Mère shook her head and pressed her lips together, urging Julienne to a faster pace. "Nothing. He is no one."

"Maman—"

"I will not speak of this here, not now. Tomorrow, *ma fille*, I will explain, but today..." She offered a smile, but it looked... frightened. Which was strange. Never in her life could Julienne remember seeing her mother frightened. "Today you must concentrate on the duc. He is expecting us."

Dread churned into nausea. And left her wondering if it was this Englishman her mother feared...or the duc de Remi.

Three

Fairchild settled on a bench within view of the stables and tilted up his face to receive the warm morning sunshine. The air was still cool and damp, and it reminded him of home. If he closed his eyes, he could imagine he sat in the gardens at his father's Hampshire estate. He could pretend he was still a boy, with no cares beyond avoiding his tutor as long as he could manage it and devising a new trick to play on his older brothers.

Sometimes he could scarcely believe that he had wandered so far from what had once been home. That he had seen the Americas, the Caribbean, the Mediterranean. That he had fought in wars, had commanded troops, had watched so many friends fall beneath the sword.

And that when he had returned to Fairmonte, it had still all seemed the same. Untouched.

He stretched out his fingers, yearning for the familiar pages of his Bible. He hadn't dared bring it with him—'twas an English translation, and he hadn't a French one. And though he would by necessity confess to Lady Poole and Lady Julienne that he was British, he could not risk anyone else discovering it. They would certainly remain silent because it was their secrets he carried. But the rest of the court…

Father in heaven, open their hearts to hear Lord Poole's plea. Help me to convince them quickly of the need for them to return to England. Clear the path homeward, please.

He opened his eyes, but still Julienne's face filled his mind. *And insulate my heart.*

She was even more beautiful without the mask than he had supposed. And not as young as he had feared. She was yet unwed, but it could bring little comfort. Not when he realized last night that the mysterious duc Lady Poole had mentioned was none other than the duc de Remi.

He had learned on his last trip here that Remi was a formidable man, one renowned for his iron fist with his tenants and feared in the political arena. While some of the aristocrats supported the idea of change for the Third Estate, the duc was not among them. He rather seemed perfectly content to prosper while others starved.

Much like he seemed content to let his wife die alone at their château while he remained at court with Julienne.

Fairchild's fingers curled into his palm now, and the peace of the morning seemed to burn away under the ascending sun. Some said Julienne was the duc's mistress—a reasonable assumption on the one hand. Others insisted she was not, that he wouldn't continue to pursue her so single-mindedly if he had already acquired what he so obviously wanted. Not that Fairchild had realized, when he first heard the gossip about the duc de Remi, that it was *his* Julienne of whom the court whispered.

But now he knew. Oh, now he knew. And nearly wished he could have held longer to the comfort of ignorance.

He had watched them last night at the meal. Watched the way the middle-aged duc fawned over her, the way he never let her out of his sight and snarled at any other man who dared to speak to her. Much as he had watched the way she avoided the duc's touch whenever she could manage it, the way she moved her feet in a constant dance to evade him, all while making it look as though she were merely playing the flirt.

She wasn't. Nay, she was rather parrying him like a swordsman, so expertly that the duc seemed oblivious to the nature of her moves. But Fairchild understood.

Unless, of course, he had merely convinced himself of what he wanted to believe.

"*Bonjour*, monsieur."

Her voice brought him to his feet. It tugged a smile onto his lips. He swept off his hat and made a quick bow, noting she was dressed to ride but alone. "*Bon matin*, mademoiselle. Is your mother not with you?"

She waved a hand toward the palace, the sunlight tangling in her hair and rendering it gold through its alchemy. "She is but a minute behind me. Monsieur, I…" She swallowed and stepped closer. Though her face was every bit as controlled as the mask she had worn the night they met, her eyes seethed with thought and feeling. "I owe you an explanation."

He swallowed past the dual desires to deny it and demand it as he put his hat back on. "Do you?"

She nodded and affected a pleasant expression even while her eyes bespoke sorrow. "I can only imagine what you must think of me. The presumed betrothed of a married man, one who slips away with another for a midnight stroll through the garden..."

"*Arrêtez.*" He barely kept himself from reaching for her hand—only the other aristocrats milling about the grounds halted him. "Please, stop speaking of yourself so. I know..." Caution stilled his tongue. Any one of the people nearby could be the duc's ally. He didn't dare breathe a word against him.

The turn of her lips mocked the sheen she blinked away. "It is an honor to have gained the duc's attention. One I certainly neither expected...nor sought."

What could he do but nod? 'Twas as he had thought. Remi had decided she would be his, and she had not been consulted on the matter. His throat constricted when he considered what the duc might have done to her had he caught her with Fairchild that night in the garden. Innocent conversation would not have looked so innocent to a jealous suitor.

Though let the man try something when *he* was present— let them see how the life of a coddled noble bore up against twenty years of military training.

She drew in a deep breath and moved to his side, nodding toward Versailles. "Here comes Mère."

His hand yearned to settle on the small of her back. To guide her forward, to protect. To pull her close, to embrace.

To distract himself, he followed her gaze and spotted Lady Poole coming their way, dressed in a stylish riding habit with a crop in her hand. Though he could not yet make out her face, he suspected there would be hard lines around her mouth and eyes like the ones that had appeared yesterday. "I imagine you had an interesting discussion last night."

"*Non.* There was no time." But her tone rang now with

steel. Obviously, she needed the answers to the questions he raised yesterday. Well, he would see that she got them.

Once the countess joined them with a *bon matin* full of false cheer, Fairchild motioned for the groom to bring out the horses he'd already asked to be readied. He helped the ladies up onto their sidesaddles and then swung onto his mount. He nodded at Lady Poole. "I defer to you, madame. Where shall we head?"

She didn't so much as meet his eye. Nay, she adjusted her gloves and picked up the reins as if he scarcely earned any regard. "A ride through the countryside would be just the thing today, I think."

He nudged his horse into a trot when she did. And, when Julienne fell in beside him rather than her mother, he couldn't resist sending her a smile. "I am curious. Does the duc know you are out riding with me this morning, mademoiselle?"

Lady Poole looked over her shoulder with narrowed eyes. "We naturally told him that you were an acquaintance of my late husband to whom we must pay our respects, monsieur. He himself was a friend of the comte de Rouen, so he understood."

"Ah." Fairchild schooled his lips into a proper expression of near boredom. "Very good. I feared I might cause you some disquiet. Last evening at the court meal the duc seemed very… protective."

"Of course he is." The countess raised her chin. "My Julienne is a prize coveted by many, and he knows well how fortunate he is to have won her heart."

Julienne made no response other than a too-quick exhale that someone more cynical than he may have called a snort of derision. Her fingers tightened on the reins but then immediately relaxed. Otherwise, her face remained clear.

Evidence enough that she dismissed her mother's words as false. A young woman in love would have smiled.

They made only idle conversation for the next ten minutes as the countess led them past the gardens and hedges, past all the people meandering about. Past, even, the drilling regiments on the green that made Fairchild take note as much as they had yesterday.

Then, finally, open countryside surrounded them, where no listening ears could hide. And the countess pulled back to fall in on her daughter's other side. The look with which she speared him was anything but warm. "Now speak, monsieur. Tell me why you have dared to intrude upon my peaceful life with your absurdity."

Fairchild tried to hold her gaze, but his eyes shifted of their own volition to Julienne. She watched him intently, but no accusation came from her. He drew in a long breath and looked to her mother again. "Your life will likely not be peaceful much longer, madame. You are insulated here at Versailles, but I have been all through France, and the things I have seen… Already the Third Estate has taken its first stand in demanding a constitution. They will not stop until they have demanded equality, something rarely achieved without the shedding of blood."

For a moment she stared at him as if he spoke in Russian rather than French. Then she let out a scoffing laugh. "The peasants? You speak to me of ghosts because of the distress of the *peasants*? *Mon chére*, you worried me needlessly. That will be resolved quickly enough. The king has it well in hand."

"No, he does not. And when I brought word of the state of French affairs home, I was not the only one who thought uprising and riots were sure to come."

"Home." Julienne's voice trembled over the word, and her fingers now gripped the reins as if they were all that anchored her to the world. "And where, monsieur, is home? Ushant?"

He granted himself only a moment to wish there were some truth that would not be so bitter for her. "London."

Lady Poole drew in a sharp breath. "The state of France is no business of the British!"

That drew a dry laugh from his lips. "Comtesse, when have our nations not been of the utmost interest to each other? Eager to find some way to gain the upper hand? It has always been so—even when you married the Earl of Poole some twenty-six years ago."

"I do not know—"

"Mère! Why do you bother denying it? Our presence here says clearly that you know exactly of what he speaks." Julienne wore fury well. It made her look more the elegant woman and less the *ingénue*. Though when she turned her face toward him, it softened to determination. "Tell me who this man is."

"No." Her mother reined in, and they followed suit, halting. "No, you will not hear the story from a stranger's lips. It is mine to tell, not his."

He acknowledged that with an inclined head. "Then by all means, my lady," he said in his native tongue. "Tell it."

The way her chin quavered, he nearly regretted forcing her hand. Never in his life had he deliberately brought a woman to tears—but it must be done. 'Twas for their better good.

She focused her gaze on her daughter. "I was only seventeen when I became engaged to the comte de Rouen. Our wedding was still some months off when he inherited a sizable plantation in the Caribbean, and he decided to travel there to assess it."

Julienne sighed. "I know this story already, Mère. What has
it to do with a British—"

"I will get to that part." Lady Poole squeezed her eyes shut.
"He enjoyed life on the plantation and requested I join him
there. So my parents and I traveled to Martinique. We were
married, and my family promptly returned to France."

When the countess's voice broke, Julienne drew in a long
breath and reached over. Her mother took her hand with a
small smile. "Then the comte died, as you know."

"*Oui*, only a month into your marriage. And you stayed a
while longer and then came home."

"*Mais non*. I did not stay at all." Her mother looked away,
toward the horizon. "I hated it there, and I had no great affection
for either the comte or his family residing on the plantation. I
boarded a ship immediately. But we were only a few days from
port when we were set upon by..."

"The British." Fairchild put in when it seemed she would
not continue. "Specifically, by one Captain Gates, then a second
son to an earl and determined to make his fortune on the seas."

The lady's face combined whimsy with pain. "It was a love
like lightning, bright and startling. We married in Barbados,
not caring about all the reasons we ought to have waited."

Though Julienne's gaze left her mother's face for only half a
moment, it was long enough to meet his, long enough to echo
the questions that reverberated inside himself. Was that what
they had experienced that night—a lightning love? Bright, yes.
Startling, definitely. But was love the proper word?

Maybe. Yes. But it hadn't been so fierce as lightning, nor
so quickly gone. It hadn't led them to any hasty decision that
night but rather to months of wondering what might be.

"We were foolish. And soon realized it." Lady Poole sighed

and looked to her daughter again. "A letter was awaiting Edward in Barbados, from his family—news that his brother had died and he was now an earl. We sailed directly for England."

Julienne swallowed and drew in a breath whose quavering strummed on Fairchild's heart. "And this man is my father? Not the comte de Rouen?"

"Without question, yes. He was a good man, Julienne. Do not think otherwise. He tried to prepare me for life in England. But I… For a year I tried, but his mother and sisters hated me, his sons—"

"Sons?" Julienne's hand slipped out of her mother's.

Lady Poole sighed. "Yes, from his late wife. Two of them."

"Brothers." Incredulity saturated her tone, but it bore the tone of joy. "I have brothers?"

"They never accepted me, certainly not as their mother nor even as a friend. And it became worse after you were born. The dowager countess tried to take you from me. She told me I must send you to live with a nurse until you were weaned." The lady shook her head. "Your father was no help, being too overwhelmed with the estates he knew nothing about. I wanted home. I wanted my père. So I told him I was going to France for a visit, and I…never went back."

"Maman!"

The word was a plea, for what Fairchild could not be quite sure. For understanding, perhaps, or compassion.

Lady Poole's face reflected back the same need. "I intended to, Julienne—at first. But things all looked so different once I was home again. That life seemed so very far away. And Père, he refused to acknowledge that Edward was my husband and told everyone I had only just left Martinique. No one questioned it. And because you were a girl and Rouen's estate had already gone to a male heir, I saw no harm…"

Julienne slid off her horse. She was silent, her face blank again, but Fairchild swore he felt her ache, felt her grasping at composure, at calmness for her mother's sake. He dismounted too, though he made no other move when she walked only a few steps away and halted. At Lady Poole's motion, he absently assisted her from her saddle.

The countess pressed a hand to her temple. "What is it Edward wants, monsieur?"

Fairchild looked from her to Julienne to the countryside. Somewhere out there, peasants could be rioting even now. Taking what their lords refused to give to keep their children from starving.

And were they not, would Lord Poole ever have made a move to regain the wife and child he had lost? Only God in heaven could know.

"He wants his wife and daughter back, my lady. A chance to prove to you that your love was not so fleeting, and to get to know Julienne. More, he wants you to be safe and fears, as I do, that France will not be able to keep you so much longer."

Lady Poole was shaking her head long before he finished. "*Non*. I cannot just uproot us from our life. This is all Julienne has ever known. She is betrothed. We cannot—"

"Mère, stop." Julienne turned to face them, her countenance as intent and beautiful as any granite statue in the grotto. She raised her chin and met Fairchild's gaze. "I will go."

Four

Mère's mouth went slack as her eyes reflected disbelief, even alarm. But Julienne scarcely felt the sway of that. How could she, when this beautiful man stood before them and offered her everything for which she had been praying?

Escape. A new life. A chance to be someone other than the duc's presumed mistress. And maybe, just maybe, to be something more besides. A daughter. A sister. And perhaps someday, if it was what the Lord willed, loved by a man who saw her heart.

"Julienne, *ma fille*, you cannot know what you say." Mère reached out toward her, but she shook her head.

"I am not a child, Mère. I am five-and-twenty. I have been engaged, jilted—"

"You were *not* jilted." Mère's face went hard and pale. "Do not say such things."

Julienne stepped to the comte's side. "I would have been, had François lived long enough." She looked up at him and found his gaze compassionate and a bit disbelieving. Her breath caught, her pulse sped. "I daresay we needn't fear any gossip from the comte. He...wait. Who are you really? Not Charles Mercier, I suspect."

He swept his hat off his head and bowed. "Isaac Fairchild at your service, Lady Julienne."

Issac. *Oui*, it suited him better than Charles. She smiled and extended her hand. And tried to wrap her tongue around English words, though she hadn't spoken them much since her days with her governess. "It is a pleasure to meet you. It seems I am Julienne Gates."

His fingers closed around hers. "The pleasure is all mine, my lady."

What was it about his hands that made her never want to let go of them? What was it about *him* that made her want to nestle into his side and hide her face in his broad chest? Surely if she did, nothing else would matter. The duc would cease to be. The rest of the world would fade away.

"Julienne, *non*." The horror in her mother's voice brought her gaze over—and she suspected it was no longer her declaration that she would go to England to which Mère objected. "You do not know this man. You—what exactly happened between you two at this masquerade at which you met?"

"Nothing, my lady," Fairchild said with ease, a calming smile teasing those dimples out. "We shared one dance. Then a promenade through the garden."

And fell in love. Julienne saw no point in denying it to herself any longer, not when he was by her side again. For the first time in far too long, the sunshine brightened her heart and the birdsong made her want to dance.

Mère hissed out a slow breath. "Julienne, what is the matter with you? You are affianced—"

"I am not." Her fingers tightened around Isaac's, and his

returning squeeze lent her confidence. "How could I possibly be promised to a man not free to give one? I have never wanted to marry the duc, Mère, never. And I will not. Not now that I have a choice."

Her mother shook her head with so much vigor that she had to reach up to anchor her hat. "Listen to yourself. You would cross the duc de Remi? You must not, or we will all pay."

"Not if we are out of his reach. Maman, if we go to England—"

"I cannot!" The shout and wide eyes made her mother look more like a child than an esteemed matron of the court. More like a frightened bride than a widow.

Julienne released Isaac's hand so she could wrap her arms around her. "You can. You yourself said he is a good man. And he wants you back."

"*Non*. He does not. I said things to him in my last letters he will not have forgiven. Made accusations...no. It has been too long. It is too late."

"My lady." Fairchild held out a hand, palm up in a gesture of pleading. "If all wrongs had not been forgiven, if it were too late, then he would not have begged me to risk a second trip into France to convince you to come home. He has regrets too—many, I would guess, though he did not share them all with me. But he did say his greatest one was not coming after you sooner and missing so many years of your lives." His gaze locked on Julienne's again. "And he expressed the deepest yearning to know his daughter."

She gave her mother a squeeze. "I want to meet him. I want to know my father. This is an opportunity I never thought I would have."

Mère pulled away and swiped at her eyes. "You speak as

if it were so very simple. As if there were not a lifetime to be bridged, as if one of the most powerful men in France were not determined to marry you. As if we could leave with no consequences."

Bitterness pounced and fought for control of Julienne's tongue, making her want to point out that, no, leaving *always* had consequences, as her mother should have known twenty-five years ago, but she bit back the words and drew in a steadying breath. "I am willing to accept whatever comes from it."

"Julienne."

She shook her head again at the surprise in her mother's tone. "All my life I have done exactly what you instructed, but I intend to do this with or without you. Know that as you consider your decision."

"You baffle me." Indeed, Mère frowned as she studied her and then Fairchild. "I never thought you prone to rash decisions. You cannot say within minutes of hearing a story that you will leave with no thought, no prayer. Not when it could well mean your life—socially, if not literally."

How could Julienne explain that she *knew* this was the answer to her prayers without making her mother think her as impulsive as *she* had been in marrying Julienne's father?

She opened her mouth to try, but Isaac spoke before she could. "I am the first to grant the need for thought and prayer," he said quietly, "but I beg you to think and pray quickly. France is ripe for uprising, and getting you to England will be difficult enough without that added to the mix."

Mère's hands raised in exasperation. "And so we should simply trust you? You, a total stranger? You could be a pretender claiming a false association with my husband, a pirate wanting to ransom us, a murderer interested only in luring us out here alone so you might—"

"Mère!" Julienne settled her hand on Isaac's arm to comfort him, to assure him she believed no such nonsense. Though when she glanced at his face, he seemed more amused by the suggestions than offended.

He tilted his head and smiled. "I have faults aplenty, madame, but I must say this is the first anyone has thought to wonder if I am a pirate or his like."

Her mother gave him a glare that had shriveled many a man in the court. Fairchild, however, did not so much as flinch, even when she added that low hum that sounded as though she were finding every imaginable flaw. "Then what are you, monsieur? Other than a spy."

"I am *not*—" He came to an abrupt halt and drew in a quick breath. The muscle under Julienne's hand tensed. "I am not a spy by profession. I am the grandson of a duke, the son of an earl."

Her mother arched a single, deadly brow. "*First* son?"

Isaac parried the arch with one of his own. "Third."

"So you have blood but no rank." The wave of Mère's hand made it seem as though that alone were reason to distrust him.

Yet he smiled again. "I have a rank, my lady. Though I doubt it will endear me to you. 'Tis brigadier general."

Army? That ought to strike fear into Julienne's heart, the realization that he had no doubt felled some of her countrymen, that he wore the uniform of her nation's arch enemy.

But how could it, when she looked up into his face? *Non.* It would take a man of honor to rise to any rank of general, even a lesser one. Not to mention that his nation was also half hers, even if she had never realized it. He knew her brothers—

brothers! And her father. He had risked his life to come here for them.

Her mother seemed none too impressed. "Why would you be playing the spy then, monsieur? Surely it is beneath you, if you are what you say."

Fairchild shrugged. "The request that sent me here some months ago was such that I could not refuse it."

"Why?"

"For reasons I cannot disclose."

Mère huffed. "Who made it of you?"

His smile faded. "I am not at liberty to say."

"Tight-lipped, are you?"

Now sobriety took over his features, making him look wiser than his years. "I have learned the hard way to be so. Please, Lady Poole, I know you have no reason to trust me. But do pray, consider it. And take this." He reached into his overcoat, withdrew a thick envelope, and held it out. "From your husband."

Oh, the look on her mother's face. Wonder joining with incredulity, caution swirling with hope. She traced a fingertip over the front as if it contained the secret to happiness.

Perhaps it did.

Julienne linked her hands over Isaac's arm and watched the parade of feelings flit over Mère's face for a long moment. A smile tickled her own lips. Many times over the years, the topic of remarriage had come up for her mother, a handsome woman still quite young. But always she had refused. Now Julienne understood why. She had a husband, one time had not obliterated from her heart despite the distance she had chosen.

Clearing both her throat and countenance, her mother tucked the letter into the pocket of her skirt and straightened her shoulders. "I shall indeed think and pray. But for now, we had best return."

Had there been any logic to it, Julienne would have suggested they instead keep riding, through the countryside and the towns until Versailles was far behind them, until she could see freedom lapping along the shore.

But that wouldn't do. So she merely exchanged a smile with Isaac and released him so he could help Mère onto her horse and then Julienne onto hers. His hands lingered a moment on her waist, and he looked about to speak.

"Let us hurry back," Mère mother said, her voice once again controlled and even.

Fairchild only gave her a fleeting smile and moved to mount his horse. The ride back was far too quick, the crowds around them again far too soon.

Julienne ought to be used to the droves of people after so many years among them. In the last seven years she had scarcely left Versailles, lest her reputation get trampled beyond repair by the gossip that would spring up if she indulged in the privacy of Grandpère's château. Often the lack of solitude grated, but never had it made her want to flee the way it did now when they trotted back to the stables.

She wanted life again. Her own, not this shadow she had been living. Not this mask she had been forced behind. Her gaze swept over the too-familiar palace grounds. So much it had to offer—apartments and gardens, tennis courts and stables, ballrooms and libraries. But would she miss it, if she went to England?

Non. She might miss the château and the days of childhood long since put behind her. She might miss a few of the friends that remained steady and true. But not Versailles. Not the court.

Certainly not the duc.

Isaac's hands slid around her waist before she was even aware of the horses having stopped. But his touch brought her back to the present, and she smiled into his eyes as he helped her down.

"I will convince her," she swore in a low murmur when her feet touched the dirt. "Though it may take a few days."

One corner of his mouth pulled up, and one hand lifted from her waist and moved as if to smooth back a curl that had come loose, though he halted before actually touching the lock. "I expected you would be the more difficult one to convince."

She only smiled and moved to walk past him, careful to time her words just as she was nearest him on her way by. "Will you meet me tonight?" The need to speak with him more, to be with him again without pretense, burned so hot it set an ache in her chest.

Never in her life had she planned a tryst with a man, even an innocent one. And with any other man, she wouldn't dare, lest he think it an invitation for more than intended. But Isaac was not any other man, and she knew he would not make such assumptions. Especially given the impossibility of speaking with him frankly through normal means.

He looked long into her eyes, nodded, and mouthed the word, "Midnight."

No need to specify where.

All her skill at stoicism was required to keep from smiling as she swept by and joined her mother, though Mère must have seen something in her face, given the weary sigh that accompanied her probing gaze.

"Julienne, take care as to why you are inclined to the decision you are. Whether it is because you believe his warning, because you wish an acquaintance with family…or if it is something far more foolish swaying you." Mère linked their arms together and leaned in close. "Please, *ma fille*. Do not set your heart in that direction. It will only end in disappointment. You are still the daughter of a comte. You must not marry an impoverished officer."

An invisible hand took hold of Julienne's throat. Always, always she was bound by what she *must* do. When would she ever be able to do what her heart said was right? Fearing tears would choke her if she opened her mouth, she made no reply.

She was glad she hadn't given them reign when a familiar contingent approached, their coats all the height of fashion, their postures all confident and sure. Their figures ranged from too-thin to too-round, gangly to stocky.

And in their center strode the duc de Remi. Though no more than average in height or build, there was no doubt he was the most powerful of his company. He wore his authority as one would a cloak, visibly yet absently.

Julienne's fingers curled into her palm, and her nails bit her flesh in an attempt to keep the churning of her stomach at bay. He was a handsome man, if every bit as old as her mother. Clever, if without compassion. The other young women all whispered about how well *they* would receive his attention— and how they failed to understand why he had set his sights on Julienne.

He set his sights on her anew now, a smile possessing his lips that would have sent tingles through her had it come from Isaac. But from Remi, it lit a fuse of fear. Still, she gave him the smile she always did, warm but a bit reserved. Mystery, Mère had always said. Nothing drew a man like mystery.

Obviously, she knew of what she spoke. Even Isaac had first been drawn to Julienne when she was a nameless woman behind a mask, had he not? But oh, how tired she was of never being who she was. How she wondered, these days, if there was anything left of the girl she had been when she first came to Versailles.

As the duc's group joined them, Julienne held out her hand as expected, and Remi took the fingers Isaac had so recently held and pressed his lips to them. She barely repressed a shudder. "*Bon matin,* duc."

"*Ma chérie.*" He lowered her hand but held it tightly—too tightly. "You had a pleasant ride, I trust?"

Was that suspicion in his eyes? *Non*...but it was purpose. She inclined her head. "The morning is pleasant, though I would wish the company had been yours." Would wish it, anyway, were she the devotee he thought her.

"Soon, *mon amour,* our every day will be spent together." He ran his thumb over her knuckles. "I just received word that my wife has breathed her last, may God give rest to her soul."

Lord God, help me! She could only pray her face reflected what it should, and not so much as a hint of the ice that flowed through her veins. But words—they would not come. All she could do was open her mouth and blink at him.

Praise be to *Dieu,* Remi seemed to expect nothing more. He kissed her hand again. "I know. So long...it is finally over. Her suffering and ours. I must repair to the château at first light tomorrow to see to the funeral. She has no family left, so it will be a small, quiet affair. I will be gone a week at the most. And when I return..."

Her life would end—or all pretense of freedom, at the least. If she did not escape, did not go to England, he would force her to wed him upon his return, mourning period be hanged. He had already made as much clear. Given that his wife had been out of her mind for years, neither recognizing anyone nor capable of a coherent conversation, everyone accepted that he had already mourned.

Mère's arm slid around her waist, and the small squeeze she gave Julienne was exactly what she needed to find her voice. "I will miss you while you are gone, Remi."

His gaze burned into her like a torch. "And I you, *mon amour*. But it shall not be for long, and then never again." That firebrand of a gaze swept down her, as if already he possessed her, already she were his. Then he released her hand and bowed, sending a wave of relief through her. "Now if you will excuse me, I have much to arrange before I depart in the morn. I will see you this evening, Julienne. Comtesse."

Her mother pulled her onward toward their apartment while the duc continued in his set course. Julienne had all she could do to remain upright.

One week. She had one week to convince her mother of the need to escape Versailles before the duc could return and force her into the role of duchesse.

Five

The midnight moon hovered overhead like a great silver disc, full and brilliant. Fairchild tilted his face toward it, even though its gilding couldn't reach him here in the shadow of Apollo's cave. The stone was cool against his hands, soothing some of the nervous fire in his stomach. Still, each trill of a nearby nightingale sent his pulse galloping.

Where was she? Had she been unable to break away from the duc's throng? News of his wife's death had been the subject of all the gossip that afternoon, and the whole court had seemed determined to pay their respects to him at the meal that evening. Julienne had sat silently by his side the entire time, her face pale but lovely, her lips never making a reply to anyone.

But tongues aplenty had been wagging about her. About how glad she must secretly be despite her somber show. About how the wedding would no doubt take place within the fortnight. About whether she had really held off the duc all this time or if they would merely be legitimizing a relationship long-since consummated.

Fairchild pushed off the faux cave wall and paced five steps.

Try as he might to tell himself her relationship with Remi was no concern of his, it was a lie, blatant and glaring. He could not suffer the thought of her in his arms—especially knowing now how loath she was to be there.

But it would be better when it was someone other than Remi, would it not? When it was some English nobleman courting her and then taking her hand. One of a rank worthy of her father's, with an ancestral estate on which he could situate her, with family gems and secure fortunes. That, certainly, was what she deserved. For no matter how high up the ranks he might rise in the army, Fairchild would never be his eldest brother, never an earl, never the possessor of Fairmonte. Never able to provide for her as her family would expect.

Soft footfalls sounded from the path, and Fairchild turned that way just as Julienne stepped into the clearing. She must have spotted him at the same moment, for she flew past the pond and its bench and straight toward him.

Why did it feel as though he had lived this a thousand times? Why did his arms open without his conscious command, and why did they close around her so confidently when she surged into them, as if this was how they had always been meant to be?

Nay, 'twas foolishness, he knew that. Still, he pressed his lips to the top of her head and pulled her back into the grotto's shadows with him, his arms refusing to loose their precious captive. And she held on, let it be noted, and buried her face in his chest.

"You would have heard." Her voice was barely audible, which was no doubt best.

He positioned his lips just over her ear so he might make his reply no louder than a breath. "Of course. But it means he will be away. It may make it easier for you and your mother to leave."

"If she will. She would not speak to me this afternoon. She just stayed closeted in her chamber with the letter." The way her hands fisted in his waistcoat and her cheek pressed to his chest made his heart thunder. Surely she would hear it, would realize he was not unmoved by her closeness.

He ought to pull away, at least a little. 'Twould be better for his peace of mind, better for the relationship they must establish of mere guardian and sojourner.

Yet was it not safest to whisper like this? "She must, and soon. I will get you away from here, Julienne, away from him before he returns."

A shiver worked through her, and he trailed his fingers up her back to soothe it away. She let go of his waistcoat and slid her arms around him.

How was it that a sliver of heaven could find him here, of all places, when danger could pounce from any side?

"Isaac..." Again her voice was the softest of sighs. "Tell me it will be well. That the trip will be quick and my father and brothers will receive me happily. That English society will not hate me for being raised French."

"How could they?" His fingers reached for the curls tumbling artfully over her shoulder and tangled in them as he had forbidden them from doing earlier. He found her hair as silken as he had expected. "There will no doubt be some bumps, as there always are. But it shan't take much for them to see that you have everything they most admire. Beauty and wit. Good blood and excellent connections. All the young ladies shall be eager for your friendship, and all the young lords will be vying for your hand."

The tips of her fingers brushed along his jaw and bade him turn his head. He obeyed them so he might find her eyes, luminous and striking even in this low light. Though now her lips were but a whisper away. Too tempting, too alluring. But she mattered too much for a simple, quick indulgence.

When she drew in a breath, he heard a quaver. "I do not want any of the young lords."

His arms tightened around her, though he commanded them to relax again in the next moment. Much as his heart might thrill at her implication, 'twasn't a matter of what they wanted. "Your mother will certainly want one for you—and your father too, no doubt. You are the daughter of an earl."

"And you are the son of one, *oui*?"

He closed his eyes and rested his forehead against hers. For the families of so many other young ladies, his pedigree would be enough to earn him approval. Why must he always fall for those for whom it did not? First Winter, whose family had decided she ought to wait for the richer Bennet Lane. And now Julienne, whose family would aim for a titled match. "I am not enough—"

Her hand rested on his cheek. "You are everything. I dreamed of you every night, imagined a million times that you had come back. That you had found me somehow."

"I dreamed a million times of the same, and yet I feared that if ever I did find you, you would be out of my reach. And so you are."

"*Mais non*." Her hand pressed more firmly. Her tone bespoke fervor. "It need not be so impossible, Isaac. My father obviously trusts you and respects you or he would not have asked you to come here on his behalf. Surely—*non*. You are not married already, are you?"

"No." He pulled away just enough to capture her gaze again. "Never."

She shook her head, relief and bewilderment dueling for a place in her eyes. "I cannot fathom how that could be. Surely the young ladies all swoon when you enter a ballroom."

A grin tugged at his mouth. "To be sure. I leave piles of fainting females in my wake wherever I go."

"I knew it." She smiled, though it lasted only a moment. "There has to have been someone at some point who stole your heart, *non?*"

He sighed and toyed with the curls still wrapped around his fingers. "A decade past, an American girl. During the Revolution. She came from a fine Loyalist family. She was beautiful and cheerful."

Compassion welled in her eyes. "What happened?"

"She fell in love with another. And, as it turned out, she was not as loyal to the Crown as her guardians were, but she and her husband remain dear friends of mine. All worked out there as it needed to." Which of course made him ask the question yet again—had the Lord led him all along to this place, this woman? Yet if he again had to face losing the one he loved because of a more appropriate suitor…

Julienne, at least, seemed to feel as strongly as he did. Winter had been fond of him but never in love with him. This would not be the same, even if he inevitably lost her.

Not the same at all. It would no doubt hurt even worse, because he would see her unhappiness.

"I cannot imagine why she would choose another, though I am grateful for it." With a small smile, Julienne leaned into his hand.

Heaven help him, but he was sinking even deeper. Why,

why must love happen again here? Why not in some drawing room in London, where he was well received and the obstacles would be few? "And what of you? How have you remained unwed when you are so lovely and highborn?"

When she sighed, he almost wished the question unasked. Almost. "I was betrothed once, but François's interest was only in my face and my dowry. I did not realize it. Not until a month before the wedding, when I caught him in an embrace with one of my friends. At which point he laughed at me for thinking he had ever loved me. It was my friend he had loved all along, and as she had just inherited a large sum, he said he intended to end our engagement and marry her instead."

Fairchild winced. Perhaps in a way it was similar to his story, but Winter had never been cruel. She had done her best to spare his heart. This François seemed to have deliberately trampled Julienne's. "I can imagine how that hurt."

She gave him a bittersweet grin. "I was less hurt than angry. I believe I said something about my grandfather not making a pleasant enemy, so perhaps he ought to think twice about his decision."

He couldn't resist chuckling. "A well-placed threat, to be sure."

"I had not even spoken with Grandpère yet when I received word that François had been killed on a hunt." She shook her head and cast that glacier gaze to the distance. "Angry as I was, I did not wish such a tragic accident upon him. My friend, she...she was devastated but could not admit why. And there was I, mournful but not as everyone supposed. Still, I was glad for the excuse to remain apart from society for a while."

"I imagine. And then, when your mourning was over... the duc?"

"*Oui.*" She rested her head against his chest again. "He returned to court just as my mother insisted I attend the balls again, and his interest was quick and clear. No one else would ever dare speak for what he had claimed, and so here I am. Five-and-twenty and very, very grateful to be yet unwed."

"Oh, Julienne." He knew not what else he could say and feared that if he dared say more, it would only prove him more the fool. Pound as his heart might, he could not give in to the longing for her. Her mother obviously disapproved, and her father just as obviously had never considered such an unbalanced match. How could he have? They had both thought Fairchild would be meeting Lady Julienne for the first time on this trip.

Yet his hand, when he commanded it to let go of her hair, only made it so far as her cheek before settling again. And his other arm, when he thought he had better set her away from him, pulled her closer.

And it surely helped not at all when she smiled up at him the way she did now, with passion and a pinch of mischief. "Are you never going to kiss me, Isaac?"

The chuckle escaped against his better judgment. "This is only the fourth time we have been in company. Only the second alone."

"Ah, but we must not overlook those scores of dreams."

Perhaps they did deserve to be counted since they were shared. And perhaps, since this could well be his only chance to kiss her, the folly of it could be forgiven. Surely 'twas right that he was able to embrace a woman he loved once in his life, was it not?

She was already lifting herself up on her toes, her arm had

already snaked around his neck. Perhaps because he had already lowered his head and pulled her against him.

Their lips touched in a soft caress, no demand within it. No rush, no regret could find a handhold in his heart now. There was room for nothing but Julienne, for the swell and crash of love that overtook him. He cradled her gently, yet firmly enough that when she sank against him, he held her up.

Kiss melted into kiss, deepening from want to need and from need to promise. The obstacles ceased to matter. Anything, he would give her anything she ever needed, ever wanted, would do anything he must to earn the right to hold her like this every day. To make her his wife, his love, to show her in a million such soul-searing kisses that she was all he would ever need.

"I love you." He whispered the words in her ear when finally he pulled away enough to catch a breath, and punctuated it with a kiss upon her jaw. Then another, and another, headed back for her mouth.

"*Je t'aime*," she murmured against his lips. "*Je t'adore.*"

A hundred years wouldn't be long enough, neither a thousand nor a million to show her how true were those words. For whatever reason, their souls had touched here in the grotto those months ago and had recognized then what the Almighty had known all along—that they were meant for each other. That though He led them on the strangest paths, all was worthwhile when they found each other.

Like this. Oh, praise be to heaven, just like this. He kissed her again, long and deep and without reserve, praying she would know, when finally they must pull away, that he would fight for her, that he would never let her go. Praying it would sustain them until he could convince her parents that he would be the best husband for her. Praying—

In the next second, his arms were empty. His eyes flew open even as a scream pierced the air for a single moment before being muffled by a black-gloved hand. He reached for his pistol only to realize he had left it in England. And though he had a dagger concealed in his boot, he hadn't the time to reach for it before the flash of another blade was caught by the moonlight—along with the enraged face of the duc de Remi.

Rough hands seized him, a pair on each arm, even as whoever had held Julienne released her to the duc's fury. Remi, a guttural growl ripping his throat, grabbed her, shook her, and jerked her until she landed against his chest with that wicked blade touching her cheek.

The terror in her eyes...*Lord my God, God of our ends, help us! Protect her, Father, please. Please, keep her safe!*

Calm descended upon Fairchild like the morning mist, touching every crevice of his being until he could breathe in and out with certainly. He relaxed his arms, his shoulders, his entire stance, and shifted to the belligerent, arrogant posture he had so disliked when he'd met the real comte d'Ushant half a year before. When he'd stood before the man who was a near mirror image to him and thought they had nothing in common at all.

But he could pretend. If it would save her, he could pretend.

"How dare you! How *dare* you take what is mine?" Remi pressed the knife into Julienne's cheek until she closed her eyes. "You think her beautiful? I can take her beauty with one swipe of this blade. *Then* what will you think?"

Her eyes opened again, and again he prayed—this time that she would understand exactly what he was doing. Fairchild shrugged. "What is it to me? I wanted only to enjoy that beauty for a night. It is you will have to look on her for a lifetime, so if you wish to make her hideous…" He raised his hand as if to wave it in dismissal, but of course his captor stopped him. Which afforded him the perfect opportunity to send the man—a servant, it seemed—an icy, unaffected glare.

Remi growled again, but he eased off the knife a bit, praise the Lord. "You think to *toy* with my fiancée? To use her and discard her like a common trollop?"

Now Fairchild widened his eyes, as if genuinely surprised by the man's offense. "You mean—monsieur, how was I to know you do not have such an understanding?" He tossed in a smirk and mumbled, "Every other couple at court seems to."

"*Imbécile.*" But Remi jerked his head, and his henchmen relaxed their grip, though they didn't let him go entirely. "Next time learn to whom a woman belongs before you try and seduce her."

Fairchild rolled his shoulders and shook off the servants' hands, and then he tugged his waistcoat back into place. "You can be sure I will. My apologies. I meant no harm, only a pleasant diversion."

Remi narrowed his eyes. "Your ignorance with the court is your only salvation, d'Ushant." The fact the duc knew his assumed name made Fairchild's blood run a little colder. "You owe me your life. Cross me again, and it will be *your* neck with a blade against it. Remember that if ever I approach you with a favor."

Not even daring to wonder what use the duc might envision for d'Ushant, he bowed. "I am at your service. Of course." He bit his tongue against asking what he would do to Julienne. D'Ushant would not care, so he must not seem to either.

But he barely repressed a sigh when the duc lowered his knife—and barely held back a shout when he then jerked Julienne around and fisted a hand in her hair, using it to force her against him and her head back to what must be a painful angle.

A whimper escaped her lips.

"But *you*." Remi's sneer looked as though it should drip poison. "You cannot claim the same ignorance."

Somehow, she managed to shift just enough to make her awkward position look captivating, as if she had put herself there willingly. "Please, *mon amour*. Forgive me. So long I have kept a rein on my feelings for you, my desire for you. I did not even know he was there, I was out here dreaming of you, of our wedding. When he kissed me I...I did not realize. I thought it you, part of my dream..."

Did the duc believe her? Fairchild had his doubts. Remi was too shrewd. But he let go of her hair and even smiled. "If it is I you wish to kiss, Julienne, you are most welcome to do so at any time."

Fairchild's throat felt dry as rice powder. She could hardly refuse him now, after that "confession." Were she to try it, Remi might yet use the knife in his hands. Still, even knowing that, even understanding, he felt the blade plunge into his own stomach when she simpered up at the duc and slid a hand around his neck. He felt it twist when she pulled Remi's head down and caught his mouth in a kiss passionate enough to make the servants chuckle and loose a low whistle.

Passionate enough to make Remi drop his knife.

That helped ease the pain in his gut. *Good girl, Julienne.*

One of the servants gave Fairchild a shove. "Enough of a

show for you, *non*? I suggest you leave before the duc decides you are not so useful an ally after all."

"Good advice, *mon ami*. Good advice." He turned as if he had no other care than preserving his own hide. And sent a prayer of thanks heavenward when Julienne pulled then from the duc.

He whispered something into her ear, something that made her giggle. Something that made the moonlight reflect a flash of fear in her eyes.

The second servant gave Fairchild another helpful push. He made a show of rolling his eyes and heading toward the garden path, but not before glancing over his shoulder to see that Remi was leading Julienne away, on a direct course for where his apartments lay.

And the knife was back in his hand, resting against the small of her back.

Six

By the time Remi shoved Julienne through the door of his expansive suite, she felt certain the knife had scorched its imprint into her spine. She stumbled over the fringe of the carpet and caught herself on a chair, wincing when he barked out the name of one of his servants.

What would he do? Dismiss them all so there would be no witnesses when he made good on the threat that lay beneath his whispered promise to give her far more than kisses? Then what?

Mon Dieu, protect me. Or if You will not, if this is the result of my own foolishness and it is Your will I suffer it, then insulate me. Make me numb. And Isaac, give him peace and comfort....

"*Oui*, duc?"

Remi tossed his hat to a side table. "Find the comtesse de Rouen and bring her to me. We will settle the arrangements for the marriage now, before I leave."

The servant nodded and disappeared out the door. Julienne jumped when it closed behind him, her gaze tracking Remi as he paced the foyer. He was like a panther with its prey cornered, waiting for the moment it fancied to strike.

He tossed the knife to the floor with a clatter that nearly shattered her nerves and then spun to her. She managed to seat herself upon the chair, some vain hope of retaining her dignity flitting through her thoughts. It abandoned her when he braced himself on the chair's arms and leaned over her.

How could a set of eyes such a beautiful brown be so cold, so hard? So unlike Isaac's, though the colors were within a shade of each other. The hearts behind them were a world apart.

"Would you like to try again, *ma chérie*," he said through clenched teeth, "to tell me what you were thinking? Why you would betray me?"

The truth tickled at her tongue, but if she spoke it, he would kill her and then hunt down Isaac. Even Mère and Grandpère could be in danger. *Non.* She could not hand them over to his rage like that. *Please, Lord. Please save us.*

"Well?"

She let the tears come as she averted her face. "What can I say, Remi? It was a foolish mistake, a lapse in judgment, and I am sorry."

He pushed off, straightened, and raked a hand through his hair. "Le comte d'Ushant. You would not know him, would not realize that his…trysts…got him chased away from court once before. He is a raptor, Julienne, preying on pretty young wives."

The real d'Ushant might be a complete monster, but Isaac was not. Still, she dared to draw in a breath at his words. Was he providing her with an excuse? "I did not know."

He was before her again so fast she hadn't even time to recoil before his knuckles cracked across her cheek. "You should not have *had* to know!"

A cry escaped, try as she might to press her lips against it.

Pain stabbed, radiated, and all she could do was cover it with a shaking hand.

Remi spat out a curse and spun away again. "I thought you better than this, Julienne. For three years you have held me at arm's length, quoting your morality. I did not respect your wishes all that time for *this*."

"I..." No other words would come. What could she possibly say that wouldn't make things worse?

He snatched up a vase and sent it to its death against a wall. "Faithless woman!"

Faithless? He called *her* faithless when he was the one who had wanted to make a mistress of her while his wife lay dying? She surged to her feet. "I am not! These three years I have never looked at another man, have certainly never dared speak to one lest you overreact."

"But you toss yourself into one's arms now?" He grabbed her and pulled her flush against him. His fingers bit into her arms so hard they would surely leave their marks upon her flesh, and he shook her. "Why?"

When trying to pull away failed, she instead threw herself against his chest again so that at least he could shake her no more. Though when she looked up into his face, she knew well her eyes were not the empty windows she usually gave him. "Perhaps I fear you, Remi. Perhaps I fear what a life with you will mean."

His smile was more a sneer, the hand he slid into her hair more threat than comfort. "Do as you should, *ma chérie*, and you will have nothing to fear." His fingers fisted around her curls, and again he used it to tilt her face up. "You are willful. You have hidden it well all this time, but there it shines from your eyes. Rest assured I shall break you of it, *ma belle*."

From where did the courage to smirk come? She didn't know, but it felt like a sort of victory upon her lips. "Would it not be easier to simply lay claim to a more docile female? That is your practice when your current one fails you, is it not? Simply choose another. And you are in luck this time, Remi, for we are not yet wed. You need not wait for me to die to find a better mademoiselle."

Her victory turned to ashes at the smile he gave her. "You think that is all you are, Julienne? A replacement upon whom I decided, like a pair of boots when I saw the need for them? *Non.* From the first moment I saw you, I knew you were mine. Mine, *mon amour,* no matter your ridiculous fiancé or my weak-minded wife."

Ice blew over her blood. "You did not even know me when I was still betrothed to François."

His chuckle lit fear anew within her, which crackled and flicked to life when he locked his other arm around her waist. "Know you? *Non.* But I saw you. I had just sent my wife to the château after her diagnosis, was just coming to grips with how she had failed me, when there you were in the gardens. A vision of beauty unlike any I had ever seen, with those eyes that could pierce a man through. I knew then I must have you, that you were made to be mine."

Her throat constricted at the terrible confidence in his eyes. "But…"

"But there was your precious François? *Oui,* a truth which caused me no little irritation at first. How fortunate he was so clumsy in the woods, *non?*"

He could not be implying…*non,* that was too terrible, too low even for him. To dispose of an enemy who had wronged him, *oui,* that she expected of him. But a man who had done nothing but choose a woman he later decided he wanted? She shook her head—or tried to, though his grip allowed for little movement. "*Non*, Remi, it was not fortunate. It was a terrible tragedy."

"Come now." He leaned forward and nipped at her ear before pressing his lips to her throat. The shiver that overtook her was far, far different from the one that had danced down her spine when Isaac had kissed the same spot not fifteen minutes earlier. "I could hardly allow an insolent pup like him to remain between us."

Non, non…her eyes slid shut, but the horror would not be blotted out so easily. "But Remi, he…he was not between us. He had ended our betrothal just that morning. He planned to marry my friend Lynette."

"*Quoi?*" He pulled back and forced her face up again. When she opened her eyes, she saw a storm raging through his eyes. "He would have tossed you over for *her*? Then he was too stupid to live anyway."

"Remi!"

"He was a maggot, nothing more. Forget him."

She already had in every way that mattered. But Remi, his behavior, his tyranny—that she could never forget. And must, at any cost, escape. "Does life mean so little to you?"

He arched a single brow. "Life? I think it a fragile thing. So easily snuffed out when a person does not value it enough to guard it. One stray shot from a rifle. One twist of a neck."

She swallowed hard when his fingers closed around hers.

But he chuckled. "Your neck is far too lovely to ruin, *mon ange*, unless you force my hand. Your skin far too perfect to mar." He turned her face and examined her cheek, probing at where he had struck her. She winced and whimpered and tried to pull away, but he held her tight. Made a *tsking* noise. "Look what you have done, Julienne. It will bruise."

What *she* had done?

Before she could wrap her tongue around a retort, the door opened, and Mère swept in. Her mother's gaze widened, and she rushed forward, knocking Remi's hands away so she could examine Julienne's cheek with her gentle touch.

Strange how her maman's presence could make her want nothing more than to let her knees go weak and the tears come.

"*Ma fille*, what has happened?"

Remi stepped away, his face once again the work of carefully chiseled stone that he wore for the public. "I caught your daughter in the arms of the comte d'Ushant, madame."

"Julienne, *non*." Their gazes locked, and though Julienne saw the very real outrage in her mother's eyes, she saw too the light of understanding. "How could you be so— Did he do this to you?"

Julienne covered Mère's hand with her own, hoping to soothe away the tremor she'd heard. "No, Maman." She looked past her mother to Remi.

He narrowed his eyes. "It must have been the result of the scuffle when my men pulled them apart. Naturally, I will punish whoever dared to mark her ivory skin."

Perhaps the words were spoken evenly, without any hesitation, but Mère was no fool. She pressed her lips together, worry swirling in her eyes only when her back was to the duc. They cleared just before she pivoted to face him. "I should hope so. Foolish though her action may have been, one moment of folly is hardly cause for such rough treatment. She is a good girl, my Julienne. I am sure it was a moment of weakness, nothing more. Certainly it will never happen again."

"Of that I intend to be sure." Remi strode to the cabinet against the wall and unstopped a decanter, sloshing liquor into a glass. "Julienne will not leave this apartment until we are wed."

Non. He could not hold her here, a prisoner. Julienne stumbled backward into the chair. He could not— She must convince her mother to leave France. They must rendezvous with Isaac.

Mère stormed after the duc. "*Pardonnez-moi,* monsieur— but my daughter most certainly will *not* be residing in your rooms *until* you are wed!"

Dark amusement lit his eyes as he sipped at the drink. "There will be no harm, as I will not be in them. And you are welcome to stay with her, madame. But I promise you, her lovely feet shall not cross the threshold until my return. I will have every entrance guarded. No one will come in, and she will *not* go out."

Her mother fisted her hands against her hips. "Absurd. We have much planning to do for the wedding—"

"Yes, you have, and all of it can be accomplished from here." His gaze found Julienne again. Hard, unforgiving. Determined to have what he wanted. "Commission your gown, *mon amour.* Redecorate the rooms if you so wish."

Mère huffed. "And how are we to commission her gown if no one is allowed in?"

A spark of amused respect flashed through his eyes. "Very well, I shall leave a list of approved visitors. Your father, madame, and those with whom you will need to speak for the wedding. But no friends. Most certainly no *male* friends."

Her mother raised her hands in surrender, but not without

a huff. "I feel you are overreacting, *monsieur*, but so be it. Send a servant for our things, if you will, and show us to our room."

Leave it Mère to dismiss *him*. Relief sang through Julienne's veins as she pushed herself up and to her mother's side.

The duc raised a brow. "Your rooms, you mean. I have enough for you both."

"I think not, monsieur." Somehow, her mother's smile was placating even as it was challenging. "I will indulge your lack of trust in Julienne right now, but you must indulge me in my lack of trust in you, with so beautiful a young woman under your roof."

Remi bowed, though Julienne did not miss the spark of displeasure in his eye. The chill that clawed up her spine told her Mère may have just spared her more pain this night. "Very well, madame. I cannot fault a mother for guarding her daughter's virtue. Come this way."

They followed him down a hall and into a chamber resplendent in its appointments, one whose beauty she might have appreciated had it not been a dungeon in purpose. She walked toward the window and looked out, swallowing back her panic when she saw it was far too high up to attempt an escape from here.

"I will be leaving at first light," Remi said, his voice cool as granite. "My steward will have instructions on the wedding. I expect you will have all arranged upon my return in a week."

"Of course, monsieur."

Julienne dragged in a long breath and turned back to them just in time to see the duc quirk a brow.

"Are you not going to give me a proper farewell, Julienne?"

Seeing no way around it, she went to him and let him pull her far too close and kiss her far too passionately.

Never again would he touch her—that she swore the moment he let her go. She would find a way out of this place, she would find Isaac, she would leave forever. Never, never again would his hands bruise or his words control.

He smirked down at her and brushed his knuckles over her cheek, pressing hard upon her bruise. But though she couldn't control the wince, she did not give him the satisfaction of another whimper. He tweaked her chin. "One week, Julienne. Use the time to reflect on my generosity in forgiving you."

She dug up a smile, though surely mockery tainted it. "I will dwell on little else, Remi."

He left, pulling the door shut behind him. And then she let her shoulders sag.

"Julienne." Her mother led her over to the bed and sat beside her on its edge, wrapping her arms around her. "He struck you?"

Tears clogged her throat, so she only nodded against her maman's shoulder.

"I am so sorry, *ma fille*. I never would have thought he would. He seemed to love you so."

Now Julienne lifted her head and met Mère's gaze, grasping her hands. "It is not so noble a feeling, Maman. He…" The terrible truth slapped her just as Remi had done, bringing a flash of memory. François, by no means innocent but certainly not deserving of his fate. His blue eyes, perhaps filled with mockery at their last meeting, but once held dear. Extinguished. Extinguished merely because Remi had glimpsed her. It was too terrible to grasp.

She shook her head. "He killed François. Or perhaps had another do it, I do not know, but he said…he said he was a

maggot who did not deserve to live, that he could not suffer
him be between us—"

"Hush, child, calm down." Her mother squeezed her
fingers and glanced toward the door, though Julienne had not
spoken above a whisper. Her brows furrowed. "You had not
even met then."

"I know. But he said he saw me in the garden and knew I
was his. He is mad, Maman. He must be, to think…"

"Mad on power." Drawing in a long breath, Mère squared
her shoulders. "But why, Julienne, why did you have to do
something so foolish as meet the comte? It would have been so
easy to slip away while the duc was at his château, but now…"

She tried to press her lips down against the tears. "I know.
I just…I had to see him. I…I love him."

Mourning filled her mother's eyes. "Julienne."

"At the masquerade, we wandered through the gardens and
talked for hours, and we…I…neither of us even knew who the
other was. Yet all these months we have both been dreaming of
finding each other again."

Mère muttered a prayer. "And what did the duc do to *him*
when he caught you?"

"Nothing. He threatened him and let him go."

"That seems very unlike the duc, *non?*"

Julienne shrugged and called to mind the way Isaac had
transformed before her eyes, from the gentle soul she loved
into…well, apparently into the comte d'Ushant. "It seems
the real comte is known for his conquests. He played the part,
claiming our encounter was nothing to him. Remi believed it
and apparently thought he would benefit from d'Ushant owing
him a favor."

"And you are sure *that* was the pretense?"

"*Oui.* Very sure."

But to think of the danger they had both been in, and of how it had thrown their plans into chaos…Julienne squeezed her eyes shut, but she felt her mother's hand smoothing her hair back. Heard her mother's shaky breath. "Isaac Fairchild aside, we must get you away from the duc. It will not be easy now. His guards are more loyal than the king's. But I will speak with your grandfather and with this Englishman you have such faith in, and we will find a way."

Julienne opened her eyes again, though Mère's image was blurry. "We will go to England? To my father?"

No tears could obscure the light of hope in her mother's smile. "*Oui.* To your father. He is most anxious for us to come."

Julienne laced her fingers through her mother's and held on tight. "You still love him."

Her smile went wistful. "I thought myself long since past such foolishness. But the moment I saw his script upon that page… Well, I cannot say what the future may bring for him and me, but he deserves to meet his daughter. We will go, *ma fille.* The very first moment we can arrange it, we will go."

If only they knew when that would be. Julienne swallowed and glanced again toward the window. "I am sorry it is so difficult now. This is my fault."

Her mother leaned close until their foreheads touched. "It is Remi's fault, ultimately. You were only acting the part of a love-struck fool." She pulled back again and gave her a crooked smile. "That embrace had better have been worth it."

The smile that tickled Julienne's lips just proved that even the darkest nights had a sprinkling of starlit hope. "Oh, it was, Maman. It was."

Seven

"Y‌ou are *imbéciles*, all of you." Jean-Paul then muttered something unintelligible, but no doubt just as insulting, under his breath as he repositioned his hat.

Fairchild wavered between a grin at his friend's discomfort and a scowl at the fact that he feared him to be right. Five days they had watched, waited, and plotted. Five days of an unlikely alliance with the marquis de Valence, his daughter, and a handful of servants the marquis trusted implicitly.

Five days to pull his nerves so taut Fairchild imagined they would fray and snap at any moment. He glanced over his shoulder at the silver-haired marquis, whose face bore no emotion. But he felt it, clearly. All of them did. All of them loved her, otherwise they would never take such a risk for her happiness.

Lady Poole slid to Fairchild's side, her eyes set upon the window at which Julienne sat. "We must move quickly. All is ready?"

"*Oui*, madame. The horses are hitched to the carriage and all is packed. As soon as we bring her out, we will be away and in Paris by this afternoon." Though that made his shoulders tense. The detour to Paris felt like a bad idea to him, but the countess had insisted. Their home there was where she had left her remembrances of England, and she swore that returning to her husband without them was impossible.

"Very well. Père?"

The marquis shot Fairchild a steady look. They had already had an hours-long discussion on his intentions toward Julienne, his prospects, his knowledge of the Earl of Poole and his family, and how he had become entangled in the youngest Gates's work because of his resemblance to d'Ushant. Without question, the man approved neither of Fairchild nor of Lord Poole, but he approved even less of the duc treating Julienne as he had and threatening the very lives of those he held most dear.

A classic case of one's enemy's enemy, really, but Fairchild would take it.

The marquis nodded. "I am ready. Let us get this over with."

The group exited the cover of the hedge, and the servants, all dressed in clothes befitting nobles, took up the planned nonsensical chatter. One of the maids wore a hat so ridiculous in its styling that the eye could not help but be drawn to it. And to make the group even more chaotic, they all kept stepping in front of each other to exchange a word with someone else before spinning back to their previous companion.

Perfect. Fairchild offered his elbow to Lady Poole, who tucked her hand into its crook just as they had planned. She said nothing at first, but once they entered the building that housed the duc's apartments, she took up her planned prattle about the ball that night.

Fairchild repositioned his overcoat as they mounted the stairs, needing to reassure himself that his weapons were in place. As a supposed noble, he was entitled to the sword now strapped to his side, but he would just as soon keep the pistol, borrowed from the marquis, hidden.

His heart may have wanted to speed up at the thought of seeing Julienne again, but he kept himself in check, his training at the fore. Kept his breathing even, his senses on alert. Each person they passed was a possible enemy combatant. The guards standing outside the duc's doors were the officers he intended to pick off.

Ah yes, he had learned a little something from the Americans when fighting against them. That sometimes the battle was already lost if you had to take to the field. Better to win beforehand, by wit and wile.

Their gaggle drew the attention of the guards, but in the way they had expected. With a roll of the eyes and shake of the head, the one Lady Poole had said would be in command stepped forward. "Madame, *bonjour*. May I be of service?"

Lady Poole looked up as if surprised to find the guards there and withdrew her hand from Fairchild's arm. "*Oui*. You may open the door."

While the commander sighed and focused on the countess, Fairchild slipped behind one of the maids and moved toward the second guard. His attention was also on the crowd, whose volume seemed louder than ever in the corridor, allowing Fairchild to slide up behind him.

"Madame, *s'il vous plaît*. You know I cannot allow everyone in, only you and your father. The rest must wait here for you."

"Nonsense." The countess waved a hand at the crowd. "They are needed for the planning of the wedding. We will be only a few moments, but we must speak with my daughter at once so we can proceed."

With a silent prayer, Fairchild covered the mouth of the second guard with one hand, and with the other pushed hard upon the pressure point on his neck. The man flailed, but the movement of the crowd kept that from view until finally he went lax. One of the marquis's menservants slid over to take the limp figure, pulling him into an alcove to gag him and bind his hands and feet.

Fairchild headed for the one in charge.

"…not possible. You know, madame, how strict were the duc's instructions. No one else may enter. Not even for a moment."

Lady Poole huffed. "That is absurd!"

Before the man's attention could shift from her to him, Fairchild stepped into range and leveled a well-aimed punch at his nose. Eyes glazing, the guard opened his mouth…and then crumpled before he could make a sound.

"Well, you *are* handy to have around." The countess grinned at him and pulled opened the door, the females moving en masse with her through it. No one needed a reminder to move quickly.

Another of the men had caught the first guard and made to pull him off to join his compatriot, but Fairchild shook his head and positioned himself against the door frame, listening. Sure enough, the interior guards asked a question at the women, and Lady Poole insisted the doormen had given their approval.

Careful to stay out of sight, Fairchild lifted the guard's arm and gave it a little shake to make it look as though he were waving his agreement.

"Fine, fine. But be quick."

A sigh of relief wanted to well up within him, but he didn't dare release it. Instead, he eased the door mostly closed and handed off the unconscious man to the waiting servant. From within the apartment he could hear the incessant chatter and laughter of the ladies, nothing within it to grab any particular attention.

Not until he heard the words he had been waiting for, rising above the rest. "Hush, ladies. Let us leave my daughter to nap. You get your rest, *ma chérie*, and that headache will leave you. I shall return to check on you in a few hours."

The click of an interior door sounded, and then there was a chorus of whispers—the kind that would require young women to put their heads together and so obscure their faces with the brims of their hats.

Fairchild pushed the door all the way open for the group, each heartbeat a prayer that the men inside would not bark out a sudden, "*Arrêtez!*" That they would not notice there were now seven young ladies instead of six, two in a neutral cream dress rather than one.

But they all exited without garnering such a command, and the marquis pulled the door closed with visible relief.

Fairchild scarcely noticed the crowd. His gaze homed directly in on the new addition, even as those unforgettable glacier eyes lifted and found him. Only when he felt her fingers in his did he realize he had stretched out a hand. But once he held hers, he saw no reason to let go. Nay, rather he lifted it so he might kiss her knuckles even as he pulled her down the hallway. "We must hurry."

As soon as they gained the out of doors, the maid who matched Julienne separated from them and headed back for Lady Poole's rooms. The rest headed for the stables, where the marquis's carriage waited.

Julienne squeezed his hand a little tighter with each step.

She, like him, must fear that at any moment the duc or his men would jump from the shadows with a gun aimed at her heart. But they made it to the carriage with no surprises.

One of the servants opened the door for them and helped Julienne up. Her mother quickly followed, and Fairchild took the seat across from them.

Lady Poole leaned out, her brows drawn. "Père, are you certain you will not join us? Please. I fear the duc will know you helped us."

The marquis smirked. "I imagine he will. And I imagine he knows there are some yet in the court he cannot touch, lest he lose all the power he holds so dear. I am safe from him, *ma chérie*. I'm only sorry I have not better kept my two most precious ones safe as well."

"Promise." A tremble quivered her lips. "Promise you will visit us."

"I will try, *ma fille*, if the king can spare me." His eyes, only a shade darker than Julienne's, moved to Fairchild—and hardened. "If a hair on their heads is harmed, I will kill you myself."

He sent the man a rueful smile. "If a hair on their heads is harmed, monsieur, it will be because someone else has already beaten you to it."

"We will be well, Grandpère." Julienne leaned over her mother to press a kiss to the man's weathered cheek. "*Je t'aime.*"

"*Je t'aime, ma fifille.*" The marquis turned away, but not before Fairchild saw a telltale shimmer in his eye.

His chest tightened. Why must one family be broken for another to be reunited? Why must there always be loss for there to be gain? But there was no choice, not now with the duc as an enemy. Their hope would have to be that the marquis's missing them would outweigh his loyalty to Louis. And that being forewarned, he could avoid the danger Fairchild felt certain was brewing.

The door closed, and the driver clicked up the horses. Lady Poole stared out the window at the world passing them by, but Julienne shifted to the seat beside him and turned her face into his shoulder, her eyes squeezed shut.

He put his arm around her and anchored her to his side. And his mind flew back a decade, to another trio escaping imminent danger, another face he loved turned into a solid shoulder. Not his, not that time. He had been only an observer when Winter, Ben, and Freeman fled the City of New York. An enemy, really.

One who could not bear to see his friends come to harm.

Never had an ounce of regret plagued him for helping them leave with their lives, despite the fact that General Arnold would have had him drawn and quartered had he learned of it. Some things transcended politics, just as this did. No matter if France had long been the enemy of England. The heart knew no such claims.

But man—man did. And if the wrong men caught them anytime between here and when their ship eventually reached England...

Fairchild squeezed his eyes shut and prayed.

The air felt charged as they drove into Paris, as if lightning sizzled through it. Julienne looked out the window, upward, but saw not a cloud in the sky. Why then this electricity sparking along her nerves?

Her own anxiety, no doubt. Even the soothing caress of Isaac's thumb over her knuckles could not erase the gnawing sensation in her stomach. She drew her bottom lip between her teeth and wished she weren't seeing the familiar buildings of Paris, wished they were rather headed for the port from which they would sail. She wanted only to be away.

Mère let out a startled gasp when they turned a corner. "What is going on?"

Isaac's face had gone grim. Julienne stretched to look ahead of them out the window, her eyes widening when she saw the churning crowd at the end of the street. Their shouts echoed her way, but she couldn't make out the words. "A mob?"

Isaac muttered something she didn't catch and leaned out his window when the carriage came to a forced halt. "*Pardonnez-moi,* monsieur," he said to a man rushing away from the crowd. "We just arrived in the city. Can you tell me what is happening?"

The man paused, but he looked as though he might sprint away at any moment. "The Bastille." His voice came out in a ragged pant. "They have surrounded the Bastille!"

"What?"

"Why?" Mère leaned forward, face aghast. "To free the prisoners? But there are hardly any kept there anymore…"

The man was shaking his head. "*Non, non.* There are only seven held within. It was for the arms and ammunition stored there, madame. They have demanded—"

A loud crack filled the air, silencing the man and sending him running in the opposite direction. Even over the tumult of the crowd, Julienne could hear the rattling of metal upon metal, and then another cracking thud.

"The drawbridge!" came shouts from the crowd. "They have cut the chains! Into the courtyard!"

Isaac leaned out the window. "Turn around *now!*"

It seemed Julienne's stomach twisted into a merciless knot, and all the blood abandoned her head as their driver tried to maneuver the horse and carriage around on the narrow street. She clutched her mother's outstretched hand and Isaac's with her other. She shook her head. "Has it really come to this? Rioting in the streets of Paris?"

A muscle in Isaac's jaw pulsed. "'Twas only a matter of time, my love," he said in English. "Reports of peasants rioting through the countryside have been filtering in for days, and the soldiers who have been sent to the city will have been seen as a provocation. Then with the king dismissing Necker the other day—"

"What?" She frowned and looked to her mother. "The finance minister?"

Mère's face was white as a lily. "Père said he was doing nothing to help with the financial problems, that...well, the whole ministry was reconstructed."

"But Jacques Necker was sympathetic to the Third Estate. They will not have taken well to his ousting." Isaac's face hardened still more as the carriage headed down another avenue, equally choked with fist-waving pedestrians.

Julienne watched the transformation of his countenance with an interest she knew was desperate—a clinging to something, anything other than the shouts coming from the streets. Though even apart from that, she would have found it intriguing. The way his eyes went calculating, his features somehow shifted from handsome to fearsome.

This, then, was the brigadier general. A man with lines of responsibility around his mouth and determination turning his eyes to steel. A man whose hand gripped a pistol with all the comfort a courtier's would a fork. A man who surveyed the raging masses outside his window as if able to divine exactly what they would do next.

A man she would trust with her life as completely as she trusted Isaac with her heart.

"Are you quite certain you need those items from your house, madame?"

Mère's lips quavered. "Surely the crowds will be less in that part of town."

"Assuming we can get to it." He kept his face turned to his window, his fingers poised on his weapon.

The next half hour seemed an eternity as the driver took them forward and then backtracked, trying to avoid the throngs of angry men in the streets. There must have been thousands—*non*, tens of thousands—in the avenues, their shouts angrier with each passing moment.

Cries for sympathy. Cries for justice. Cries for bread.

Bread? The knot turned to nausea in Julienne's stomach. Never in her life had she gone without a meal. How could it be that the people were starving? She'd heard Grandpère say how the nobles had all simply refused to pay higher taxes. How had the burden then fallen onto the poor?

"What have we done?" The question she whispered out was swallowed by the invading shouts from outside.

Mère seemed not to have heard her. But Isaac looked her way and squeezed her hand. "They have seen freedom won by America and have heard tales of equality and democracy. They want that too, but they fail to care that it will coat their hands in blood."

She shuddered and leaned into his side. "You were there? In America?"

He nodded, gazing out the window again. "War is ugly

business, full of betrayal and hatred and the basest of human feelings rising to the fore."

Her mother lifted her chin. "Why, then, have you made a career of it, General?"

He breathed a laugh sans amusement. "If we left it solely to those who loved it, how much uglier would it then be, madame?" When the carriage halted, he arched a brow. "Are we here?"

"*Oui.*"

"We will all go in. I will leave neither of you alone." He opened the door himself, jumped down, and then helped her mother out.

Julienne reached for him next. Even now, with fear and nerves foremost, her heart gave a little skitter when his hands closed around her waist so he might lift her down without bothering with the steps. She sent a smile up at him when her feet touched the ground, but he was looking over her shoulder.

And his eyes lit with fearsome determination. "Back in! Up, hurry!"

Too late. The duc's voice even then pierced the air, calling Julienne's name like a curse.

Eight

Time slowed to a chaotic jumble of images and sounds for Julienne. Remi, looking furious and deadly as a pagan god in some classical painting, needing only a cape to billow behind him to finish the picture. Light flashing off the swords and muskets of the four guards. The muted clamor of the mob a few streets over, creating a cacophonic symphony. Mère's scream, Isaac's shout, and the deafening roar of her own pulse.

And the litany of denial that stampeded through her mind. *Non, non, non.* He was not here, could not be here. He was supposed to be at his country estate, not his home in Paris so near Grandpère's. He could not stop them now, must not stop them now. *Non, non, non.*

Gunshots were heard in the distance. Was it her imagination, or did that horrific sound make the duc's eyes light with even more evil glee?

"Climb up!" Isaac's command penetrated her fog. He had grabbed for her mother and pushed her toward the carriage again too. Julienne turned, shaking. She wished she knew the words to curse her skirts from letting her get up quickly in the vehicle without the steps.

Remi's voice overlapped with Isaac's. "Shoot them! Kill them if you must, but *stop them!*"

Seconds later the wood of the carriage splintered just beside Julienne's head, shots ringing out and sending her reeling away. Mère screamed again.

Julienne grasped her mother's shoulders, looking frantically for the wound. "Are you hit? Hurt?"

She managed only a shake of her head through her tears.

Isaac pushed them behind him, raising an arm. Another crack, and this time one of the duc's guards fell. To Julienne's lips sprang a prayer, memorized long ago but never before so desperately needed. *"Defende nos in proelio; contra nequitiam et insidias diaboli esto praesidium." Protect us in the battle, be our safeguard and protection against the wickedness and snares of the devil.*

Remi shouted something more, but she could not hear what. One of his men had reached them, and Isaac sprang forward. A jab, a strike, and the man's weapon clattered to the ground. A knee, a punch, and the guard soon joined it.

"The house!" Mère shouted into Julienne's ear. "Go to the house."

And leave him? *Non.* She could not. Her feet would not move. Not until her mother pushed and shoved at her so that she stumbled forward. Then she saw that a servant had opened the door for them and was waving them forward.

She made it only a step before a familiar hand seized her arm, biting into the bruises it had put there a week ago. But her cry was more anger than pain, and she swung around to hit him with her other arm with all the force she could muster.

It won her only a curse and a backhanded slap across the mouth.

The metallic tang of blood touched her tongue. The bolstering wind of defiance lifted her chin.

"Idiot woman." He tried to pull her away from freedom— the house, the carriage, Isaac, Mère, who found a stick and raised it above her head—but Julienne dug in her heels. Then she thought better of it and kicked him in the shin instead. He grunted and raised his hand once more.

Then he froze when a gun pressed against his temple. "Strike her again and I will kill you. Let her go. Now."

Even had she not already been in love with him, Julienne would have sworn lifelong loyalty to Isaac in that moment. She glanced over her shoulder to see that he had laid the third guard flat upon his back, leaving only one more coming up behind the duc, who would surely not act with a pistol to his master's head. Her mother let her arms fall to her side but kept the fallen branch in hand.

Remi's Adam's apple bobbed, though he relaxed his grip on her arm only a few degrees. "I am surprised at you, d'Ushant. Since when does one woman evoke such a reaction from you when there are plenty more out there who are not so much trouble? Leave this one alone. She is mine."

Julienne pulled on her arm. "I am *not*. I have never been, and I will never be!"

"You *are*." His fingers dug in anew, and he wrenched her arm until she gasped.

Thwak. With lightning speed Isaac wielded the pistol as a club, drawing a line of spurting red onto Remi's temple. The duc released Julienne and staggered back, shouting, "Henri!"

The fourth guard folded his arms across his chest. "*Oui,* monsieur?"

The glaze over Remi's eyes looked to be half incredulity, half pain. He lifted a shaking hand to his head. "Do something. Kill him. Grab her."

Not a muscle twitched but for one in the man's face. "I think not, monsieur."

Remi's countenance contorted, though the rage looked futile in light of the trail of blood weeping down his cheek. "You *think...not?*"

Henri's face went even more blank. "My family are all on your lands. *Villeins,* servants. They are starving. *Starving,* monsieur. And you do nothing. You cannot be bothered. You are too busy poisoning your wife so you might force this poor girl to wed you."

The stick clattered to the ground as Mère covered her mouth with both hands. "Poison?"

Fury mottled Remi's face and sent the blood dripping faster. He spewed curses at Henri that blistered Julienne's ears, and then he moved into threats as to what would become of the man's family now.

Isaac sighed, switched his pistol to his left hand, and shoved a fist into the duc's face with enough force to render him immediately unconscious.

Henri moved to stand over him, staring down with stony face. "Go, monsieur. Take the ladies away. I will see to the duc."

But Isaac lifted a brow. "What exactly do you mean by that, *mon ami?* You will hand him over to the authorities for the crimes of which you seem to have knowledge?"

The muscle pulsed again in Henri's jaw. "If there is authority to be found in these times. Or perhaps I will take him to the

Hôtel de Ville and let the people confront him along with the mayor. Or better still, let him answer to his *own* people, in Remi."

Isaac lowered his pistol but shook his head. "Deal mercifully with him."

"Mercifully?" For the first time, emotion surged into the guard's eyes. Bitterness and hurt. "He has never dealt mercifully with anyone."

Isaac met it with calm regard. "True, but he is not ultimately the Master to whom you must answer."

Julienne splayed a hand over her heart. The Lord had been smiling on her when he led this man to her side at the masquerade. For surely there was none better in all the world.

For a long moment Henri made no move. Then his face softened, and he leaned down to haul up Remi. "May you stay as safe as you are wise, monsieur. Now go, quickly, before my fellows awake."

Mère turned quickly toward the house, from which the housekeeper even then rushed, a satchel in hand. "I received your missive, madame," the woman declared, out of breath. "I had it all ready. Quickly."

While her mother met the servant, Julienne turned gratefully into Isaac's side. He touched a gentle finger to her lip, regret in his gaze. "He hurt you again."

In that moment, the pain meant nothing. Not compared to the hope. "*Non, mon amour.* Nothing a kiss will not erase."

London, England
August 1789

Fairchild nodded to the servant who had led him through

the house and stepped out into the Earl of Poole's picturesque back garden. Roses sent their sweet perfume into the air, butterflies flitted, and sunshine pooled upon the cobbled path. It was a picture of peace and promise.

If only it were so. If only it extended past his lordship's orderly stone walls.

But he wouldn't dwell now on the continuing tumult in France. Nay, that was talk for other days, other company. Not here, now, the first he'd managed to get back to Poole's town home after seeing Julienne and her mother safely to him a fortnight prior.

"General Fairchild, good afternoon."

Fairchild gave a smile to the earl's younger son and reached out to clasp his hand when he drew near. The man, three years his junior, wore a crisp buff suit and a look of calculation in his eyes. That was Gates for you. "Mr. Gates, good day. I hope I am not intruding?"

"Not at all." He motioned Fairchild off the back step and then waved a hand at the garden. "The others were taking a little promenade through the posies. It is good to see you. Have you heard the latest? That the National Assembly in France has abolished their feudal system? In a single day, all clergy and nobility lost their privileges."

So much for neither here nor now. Fairchild sighed and searched the towering blooms for those ice-blue eyes he had so sorely missed. "I have heard, yes. Our timing in getting your sister and her mother out of the country was impeccable." He darted a glance at his companion. "Are they settling in well?"

Gates studied him for a moment with pursed lips and then nodded. "Quite well. My father is giddy as a schoolboy. He and Lady Poole are behaving like newlyweds. And Taunton and

Julienne act as though it is their sworn duty to make up for two and a half decades of missed sibling-hood with incessant teasing and jesting."

A corner of Fairchild's mouth tugged up. "And you?"

Gates's face reflected nothing. "They have made the family happy, and I have found nothing objectionable in their politics or beliefs." Then a light flicked behind his eyes, and his mouth curved. "I will enjoy getting to know my sister, certainly, but I prefer to play my cards closer to my chest than my brother or father."

Farichild chuckled. "That I know well enough, my friend."

"Which reminds me. You have established yourself as d'Ushant, and the Home Office could—"

"Nay." He couldn't get the word out quickly enough. "I am done with the covert, Gates."

"Oh, come now. Your country can use your service."

He lifted his brows and glanced down at the brilliant red jacket he once again wore. "My country is getting my service."

Gates grinned and moved off as the earl came into sight. "One can always serve more, General. Remember that."

Pushing that thought aside, Fairchild headed for the earl and greeted him with an outstretched hand. "Good day, my lord."

"General." Poole's eyes crinkled when he smiled and shook hands. "How good to see you. I expected you to visit again sooner."

"Would that I could have, but my duties had piled up in my absence, and this was the first I could escape them." A flash of color caught his eye. Summer blue silk, a gleam of red-gold. *Julienne.*

Lord Poole followed his gaze and chuckled. "I cannot thank

you enough for all you have done for our family. My wife and daughter have yet to stop talking of your heroics."

She moved past a break in the hedge, one large enough so that he could see her face. That she could look up and meet his gaze.

Ah, how his heart thudded to life at the way fire danced within the ice. "I would not call it heroics, my lord, but it was certainly my honor to bring them home."

The earl shifted, his posture solemn enough to steal Fairchild's attention. He found the man's gaze intent and probing. "Julienne has also said that the two of you fell in love. Tell me, General, is this true?"

She had told him that? Fairchild sucked in a quick breath and prayed for strength. In that moment he would rather face a battalion of enemy soldiers than a rejection—even a kindhearted one—from this man. "I realize I am not the suitor you would wish for your daughter. I have no title, no wealth—"

Poole's lips quirked up. "Well, I would hardly go that far. I asked a few questions when Julienne confessed her feelings for you. You are not ill-situated. And your family certainly leaves nothing to be desired."

"That is a very generous view of my circumstances, my lord." Fairchild inclined his head, his hand smoothing down the woolen jacket as his gaze went of its own accord to where Julienne flashed into view again, a smile wreathing her face. "I have certainly striven to handle my assets responsibly, and I received fine compensation for my service in the American rebellion—but still, I realize this is not ideal for an earl's daughter."

"Yet you seem to forget I spent much of my life as a younger son as well." His hand landed, warm and encouraging, on Fairchild's shoulder. "You did not answer my question. Do you love her?"

Fairchild tore his gaze away from where Julienne and her mother and Taunton emerged from the hedge and focused on the understanding gaze of the earl. Was this man honestly willing to entrust him with this most precious woman in the world? "With all of my heart, Lord Poole."

Poole smiled. "Then, given that your heart is without question one of the noblest I have ever encountered, I would be pleased and honored to give you my blessing, if you care to ask for it."

"I..." Words twisted on his tongue, too befuddled by the rampaging joy to make sense. He nodded, grinned— undoubtedly like a fool—and turned to watch Julienne's quick approach. When she was a stone's toss away, he opened his arms. She flew into them, and he laughed as he spun her around once, again, then put her on her feet and dropped to a knee. Now the words surged up. "*Je t'aime*, Julienne. More than anything. Will you be my wife?"

She clasped his hands tight and beamed hope and joy upon him with all the brilliance of the sun. And then she said the sweetest words the world could know. "*Oui*, Isaac. I will."

Author's Note

I didn't mean to like Isaac Fairchild. He was just supposed to be a convenient plot device, someone for Winter to use as an information source in *Ring of Secrets*. But the more times he appeared in that story, the deeper his character grew, and the more I—and the readers—came to admire him. Even as I finished *Ring of Secrets* in the way that I knew I must, I was already trying to decide on what Fairchild's love story would be.

Because he would have one. He *must* have one. A man so faithful and true deserved a long, happy marriage with an amazing lady. I had already planned that the heroine of the second Culper Ring book, *Whispers from the Shadows*, would be his daughter, so in my head I devised this thrilling adventure of a love story for him...and then cautiously presented it to my editorial team as a "Hey, what do you think about filling in the gaps of the family saga with a novella?" To my delight, everyone was on board, and so *Fairchild's Lady* was born!

The French Revolution is a complex and wide-spanning

conflict that I obviously barely scratched the surface of in this short little tale, but it is well remembered for the Terror that it brought to its people...a terror that had its roots in an understandable and even noble quest for equality, but which soon devolved into chaos. I thought it would be interesting to capture just a wink of this troubled time through the eyes of a soldier who had already seen one revolution, and who had learned its lessons well.

Fairchild and Julienne went on to enjoy several happy decades together, you can be sure! And they built a home that was the perfect place for their artistic daughter, Gwen. I hope you enjoy her story in *Whispers from the Shadows*, book two in the Culper Ring Series.

A Hero's Promise

One

Baltimore, Maryland
29 January 1835

Julienne "Lenna" Lane stared at the panicked runaway huddled in the dark corner of her cellar. "Not again." Transferring her gaze to her dearest friend, she tried to summon the authority her father would have had. "Freeda."

Her friend didn't so much as look over her shoulder at the bedraggled, shivering figure—woman? girl?—huddled among Mama's jams and canned vegetables. "What was I to do, Julienne? She needed help."

Squeezing her eyes shut did nothing to erase the stranger's image. Without question, she was a slave. Escaping her master, just like the others. Hiding in Lenna's cellar. Putting the entire family in danger by her mere presence, however understandable her need to flee. "We were agreed. Instead of taking an active role, we rely on our wits and—"

"Wits help nothing here." Freeda's smoke-gray eyes flashed

in the low light that seeped in from the open door. The shadows deepened the even brown of her skin, a clear reminder that in her eyes, that mysterious slave was kin in some ways. "Meaningful as your articles are, they can't save this girl now."

A slice, that terrible truth. But still, if they wanted to effect a change that would help *all* the slaves, not just the few that made it off their masters' lands... "But—"

"Lenna?"

She froze with her mouth still open to argue, her pulse doubling at the faint but familiar voice. *Jack.* Finally!

"No." Freeda grabbed Lenna by the shoulders. Panic sparked in her gaze as it had in the stranger's when Lenna came down. "You have to lead him away from here. Jack can't see her, he can't know."

"Freeda." Lenna pulled away, even as her friend's fright lit an echoing spark in her. Foolishness, that. "It is only Jack." *Only*—as if such a word should ever be applied to him.

Freeda shoved away an escaped ebony curl and shook her head. "Jack, with his unending questions. Jack, who now answers to the government. He can't see her here! Go distract him. *Please.*"

Oh, dash it all, this shouldn't be! What had become of the days when they would all run about together, the world an adventure land open before them? Her brothers, Edward and Winfield, her and Freeda, with Jack always at the head. That was what life should have been.

"Lenna?"

Heavens. Her pulse redoubling yet again until her hands shook, she grabbed up the basket of apples from the shelf and turned for the cellar stairs. Freeda was wrong. They could trust Jack with this, she knew it. Knew it...yet she shook all the more. Her friend was right, in a way. Jack was a naval officer now. He answered to a higher authority than their fathers. If he was found abetting a runaway, it could spell disaster for his career. Once in the yard, she lowered the cellar door into place. For his own good, she mustn't—

"There you are."

She squealed and dropped the basket, sending apples rolling around her feet. Splaying a hand over her galloping heart, she spun.

Jack Arnaud stood a few paces away, his brows drawn in a scowl more often seen on his father's face than his own. One that seemed suited, though, to the somber naval blue of his uniform with its shining gold epaulettes. And the hollows in his cheeks—never had she seen him so thin, or with such shadows under his eyes.

"Jack." What must have passed these last months to make him so gaunt? She would hear it all, she was sure, and where better than in her embrace? Her feet readied themselves for the launch into his arms. She had always greeted him thus, since she was a tot, through the awkwardness of adolescence, and into these past long years when he came home but rarely. Always, because she was his and he was hers and that was the way it was.

But with her first step she nearly fell over an apple, and what with squealing again and windmilling her arms and lunging to regain her footing, she hadn't the chance to embrace him in those first moments as she usually did.

At least his chuckle erased the frown. He steadied her, smiling down at her in that way of his—which nearly outshone the shadows—and then nodded toward the mess of bruised fruit. "I'll help you with that, shall I? Why were you bringing up so many apples?"

That was the first thing he said to her after nine months apart? True, she had intended to bring up a smaller basket of them with her before she had spotted Freeda and the runaway in the cellar, but *still*. She planted her hands on her hips as he bent to toss the nearest apples back into the basket.

"I have been well, thank you for asking. Not at all anxious about whether your ship would ever make it back to port, nor about the lack of letters these last two months. I have certainly not worn my knees raw from praying for you and worrying I would have to postpone the wedding yet again."

"Lenna." He paused in his crouch and stared at the red fruit as if he had forgotten its name. And said hers in a way she hated. Wearily, regretfully, chiding.

"No. Jack, please, no." Though she wished them away, tears burned the backs of her eyes. "I am sorry. I didn't mean to greet you with frustration. I meant to bake your favorite pie, to assure you I had prayed for your safety every day, to say how sure I had felt that the Lord would deliver you home to me in time. Don't delay the wedding again. Please."

He expelled a breath as he stood and let the apple roll into the basket. "I had envisioned our reunion going differently."

As had she. Her version had been absent the fugitive in the cellar, she hadn't tripped on her way into his arms, and his lips had claimed hers in one of those kisses she hadn't partaken of in nine long months, not since he last bade her farewell. Yet now her feet felt rooted in place between him and the secrets behind her. The whole world seemed to have shifted just a bit.

His smile too looked strained. He came near, wrapped his arms around her, pressed his lips to the top of her head...but then retreated again. "Why don't we go inside? I haven't been warm in months."

A weight settled on her shoulders. She wrapped her arms around her middle and gazed up into his eyes. She knew their exact shade of brown, the way amber flecked them. She knew the way they lit with laughter so readily, and how they darkened when worry overtook him.

They were dark now, and his lips were set in that apologetic line that hinted at why he wanted to get her inside for a conversation.

He was going to do it again. He would postpone their wedding, pleading a thousand reasonable excuses—that he needed more than two days to prepare for their nuptials, but with his ship so late to port, having obviously come through considerable trials...couldn't they move it back a week? After all, he would say, what was a week? Or a month or a year or two years? They had their whole lives ahead of them...

She didn't know fury well. It was at best a passing acquaintance, one she avoided whenever she could. But in that moment, when wrathful flames exploded through her, she thought perhaps it had been growing inside far longer than she thought. She kicked at one of the apples he so loved and then, when he reached for her again, slapped his arm away. "Don't even consider it, Jack Arnaud. If you cancel the wedding on Saturday, it will be for the last time. I'll not wait for you forever."

Once spoken, the words seemed to hang in the air between them, sharp and incendiary. Lenna sucked in a breath and pressed her lips together, wishing she could unspeak them. Such lies should have no place on her tongue. She would wait forever to be his wife. If he but offered one word of assurance, if he but reached for her one more time, she would leap into his arms as she always did.

Instead, his eyes snapped with an echo of her fury. "You will lay this all at my feet? Were *you* not the one who canceled the second time?"

Fire scorched her neck. "It is hardly my fault the trip from England took nine weeks that summer!"

"Nor mine that my ship left a month earlier than expected the first time."

True, but they could have wed before he left. Why had they not? Perhaps she had not yet been eighteen, but what did that matter? Now she was a breath away from twenty and still waiting for that promised exchange of vows.

Jack folded his arms across his chest. "And will you hold the last time against me? Did we not both agree that we should focus on my father's wedding instead?"

After so many years of mourning his first wife, how could they do anything *but* focus on Alain Arnaud and his Adèle, Lenna's own distant cousin from France? The match, so unexpected, had filled them all with awed joy. And at the time, it had seemed no great thing to put off her wedding in favor of theirs.

But that was nearly a year ago. "The point remains that we are all here now, with nothing else vying for our attention. We are to wed in *two days*, Jack. You cannot postpone it again with no excuse!"

His movements jerky, he bent down once more and gathered the apples as if they were his ammunition, the basket his cannon…and she his target. "Why do you assume I want to postpone again? Of course I don't. It is just that…you cannot know how terrible this trip was. I feel about to fall over, and that is not exactly the shape I wish to be in when we wed."

As the anger seeped out, the cold seeped in. A gust of winter wind blustered through the garden, rattling a few stubborn brown leaves still clinging to their branches. Lenna sank down to a seat upon the sloped cellar door, skirts and petticoats whooshing around her. "Of course not. Do what you will."

"Lenna." That tone again. He dropped the last two apples into the basket and turned to her. "How big a pie were you planning on making?"

"I was...making several. You know how Win eats." At fourteen, her youngest brother had entered that stage where they could scarcely keep him in food—or breeches that fit his gangly legs.

But Jack must have heard her hesitation. He narrowed his eyes and held fast to the basket. "Even so, you wouldn't need the whole bushel."

Perhaps her breath came out too exasperated, but what was she to do? "When I heard you call me, I grabbed the whole thing. Why is that worthy of question?"

"Why is it worthy of evasion?"

Freeda was right—Jack was far too inquisitive. "I wasn't evading, I was..." In the face of his arched brow, her cheeks went hot. "Must you call me on being flustered at hearing you?"

One of his dimples flashed along with a crooked grin. "Yes, I must, so I can earn a blush. Though it is hardly a secret that you drop everything to greet me."

No, more a tradition—one whose lack today still made her arms feel empty and strange. Her lips should be tingling now from his kiss, not dry and cold from the January wind. She should be pulling him into the house to see the wedding gifts that had arrived in his absence and let Rosie shove food at his too-slender self, not sitting here on the cellar door hoping neither Freeda nor her mysterious companion dared to sneeze.

"Come." He held his hand out to help her up. "I'll return these to the cellar for you and we'll—"

"No!" She leapt up, biting her lip against the stupidity of her quick objection. This was why she should stick with wit, satire, and a *nom de plume*—she was terrible at actual intrigue.

Jack's face turned to stone. "What are you hiding?" He sounded not only suspicious, but baffled. As if it were inconceivable that she could possibly have a secret she wouldn't immediately blabber to him.

All right, so perhaps he had evidence to support that assumption. And she didn't *want* to keep secrets from him. But this one was not hers to share.

The other was, though. She drew in a long breath and took a step toward him, away from the cellar. "You're right, we ought to go inside. I wanted to show you something I've written—"

"Lenna, what is in the cellar?"

Her chin rose of its own volition. "Nothing to interest you, as all the apples are now out here. Please, Jack. This is important."

Frowning his father's frown again, he held her gaze for a long moment and then set the basket of apples down. "You're hiding something from me."

"Yes." Did it sound as much a hiss as it felt? "And I'll be glad to share what it is as soon as we go inside. It's freezing out here, and you haven't been warm in months."

He didn't so much as blink. Was this the face he wore on board his ship as he took commands from the captain or gave them to the noncommissioned sailors? If so, she was glad not to see it day in and day out, for it bore little resemblance to the Jack she had known all her life. He drew himself up to his full height. "I will be happy to read your latest essay later. Perhaps tomorrow. But right now we have other things to discuss."

Why must he sound so cold as he said it? The frost in his tone seeped straight to her bones. If he knew, he wouldn't put it off. But then, that seemed to be his normal response to her lately. Never mind the articles that had been lighting an inferno of debate in newspapers up and down the coast, why expect him to care for that when the idea of his own wedding seemed more burden than joy? "How long this time? Six more months? Another year?"

"I only ask a week to recuperate, Lenna. Just a week. Is that unreasonable?"

No. Not at all, except that it layered atop so much else. So many years now of waiting and hoping and being put off. So long to wonder if he had changed his mind, if he welcomed the space between them, if he had outgrown his childhood devotion.

So long to amass secrets. She dug her fingers into her sides, but the boning of her corset made her spine feel no more steeled. "Do you even want to marry me anymore?"

"How can you question that?" Irritation drew a weary-looking line in his forehead. He stepped nearer, but the arms he slid around her waist remained stiff. "I have loved you all of my life. You ought to know that. You ought to be secure in it. Of all the things in this world, *that* ought to be one we never doubt."

Sliding her frigid hands up his arms, she wondered where the security was that she usually felt within them. "It's just... you don't seem eager to wed."

"I?" And yet when he pulled away, too many emotions flashing through his eyes for her to read them, she felt all the more bereft. "You are the one not acting yourself, admitting to having kept something important from me."

"And you won't grant me the fifteen minutes required to explain it to you!"

The muscle in his jaw pulsed. She couldn't remember the last time she had made him angry, the last time they had fought... and she couldn't shake the feeling that it had all gone wrong because of her. Well, perhaps not *all*, but she had somehow started this argument by greeting him with defensiveness instead of affection.

He backed up another step, his officer's mask in place again. "What's in the cellar, Lenna?"

She had started it by hiding a runaway and not telling him outright. When she swallowed, it felt as though she tried to force down a stone. "Why can you not trust me, Jack?"

"A fine question from a woman who just admitted she didn't trust *me* to keep my promise to wed her."

Lenna clasped one hand onto the opposite arm in a vain attempt to anchor herself. Despite the warm wool of her cloak, the puff at the elbow of her sleeve, she felt nothing but ice. "Is that all it is? A promise to be kept?"

"All?" Something in his tone rang of disappointment. Something in his eyes flashed with the same. He shook his head and turned toward the drive. "Have it your way. Keep your secrets."

"No. Jack!" He couldn't leave like this. He *couldn't*. They had never parted at odds, never in all her nearly twenty years. If they did now, when they ought to be knitting their futures together...

God of my end! She flew after him, though his long strides had him halfway to the corner before she grasped his arm. "Don't be angry with me. Please. I don't want to have secrets from you. It was only Freeda."

He paused, lifting a brow.

How could she feel at once so flushed and so cold? She pressed a hand to her cheek. "And a friend. Please leave it at that."

His lips stayed firmly pressed, but his eyes went thunderous.

She dropped her hand from his arm. "You act as though you have never kept a secret." He must though. A navy man could hardly go about town blathering all he knew. Was the fight against oppression that she and Freeda had engaged in so much different from him fending off pirates?

Yet somehow she didn't expect the flash of lightning that joined the thunder in his eyes. Lightning that spoke not of recognition but of…guilt.

She drew a step away. What could he possibly feel guilty for keeping from her? He knew well she wanted to know nothing of his work that was not suitable for the telling, nothing that did not concern her directly.

But there were parts of his life away from her that *did* concern her directly.

Did the wind increase, the temperature drop? Or did she just go weak in comparison? She clasped her cloak closed tighter. "What? What is it? Is there…is there someone else? Is that what you've kept from me?"

The storm in his eyes shifted, the guilt giving way to pure, lashing outrage. With only a single, angry shake of his head, he strode away.

Lenna stared after him until he'd disappeared, until she

heard the creak of the cellar door, until Freeda's fingers wove through hers, soft brown against freckled cream.

"What happened?" her friend asked in a strained whisper.

Lenna forced a swallow. "I don't know. But I think I'm not getting married on Saturday."

Two

Night cloaked them, cold and dark, and made Jack's pulse kick up. When he'd set foot upon solid ground this afternoon, he'd thought a few days of relaxation awaited him. Time to warm himself at a fire and soak strength back into his bones. But that was before Father and Thad told him of this evening's planned outing.

And before he had made a royal mess of things with Lenna.

The two elder men led the way through the winter-barren field, Thad Lane crouched low so his towering height would blend into the night. A glance beside him showed Jack that Edward Lane, who had somehow sprouted to match his father's height in the last nine months, did the same. The seventeen-year-old had not been part of the Culper Ring when Jack left, but apparently their fathers had educated him.

A move they wouldn't have made had the young man not been ready. But still, Jack could scarcely fathom that little Eddie, seven years his junior, was grown up enough for such clandestine work.

His young friend shot him a smile that gleamed in the

moonlight, as if reading his mind. Then he made a few quick gestures that took Jack a moment to process. He never had cause to use signs among his comrades at sea. *Glad you're back, Jack.*

He smiled and signed, *Me too.* Though after the strained dinner he had just escaped with the Lanes and Arnauds, his bride-to-be might wish he had been claimed by Davy Jones's greedy locker.

What was the matter with him? All these months of wanting nothing more than to come home and take her in his arms, and he managed to push her away in a five-minute exchange. He hadn't even thought it possible—perhaps that was the problem. Perhaps he had taken her love for granted. But hadn't that been part of its beauty? That it was an *always*?

"This way, boys." Thad's whisper joined the tendril of fog rising from the nearby river. He motioned them past a few ramshackle outbuildings. Little light spilled from them, though from one he heard a soulful, mournful voice singing a hymn. The slave quarters, no doubt, though most of them must still be at work inside the big house.

Crouched down, feet silent, Jack followed the others toward the golden glow shining through the windows of Matthew Newel's proud home. He had met the younger Mr. Newel a time or two but had no personal acquaintance with the Maryland planter himself, though Father and Thad must have. They both wore a mask of barely restrained disgust when Edward had said they needed to be at his home tonight.

Jack still wasn't sure why, or how his young friend had discovered whatever it was he had. But frankly, he welcomed the excuse to escape the cold shoulder Lenna had given him all through dinner, and the questioning glances it drew from her mother, grandmother, and his father's new wife. Perhaps the Lane family had always felt like his own, but he had no doubt of whose side the ladies would take if it came down to a choice. The same side Jack himself would take—Lenna's.

A dog barked from somewhere to the left, but the warning came no closer, and a voice soon echoed through the fog telling the animal to hush. Still, Jack breathed a bit easier when they reached the house with no other alarm raised. He fell in between Father and Edward, Thad in the lead. Sticking close to the wall, they went from window to window until Thad saw something of interest within. At his motion, they all crouched low under the multipaned glass.

They stayed motionless for several infinite minutes before a noise came through the glass to tell him what Thad had seen. A curse and then the slap of something upon a table. "Joshua!"

Half a minute later, he could just make out the opening and closing of an internal door. "Yes, Father?"

"Has she been found?"

Silence stretched and crackled. Was that a mantel clock Jack heard ticking, or just his imagination? Joshua Newel cleared his throat. "No, sir. No sign of her. We lost her trail once she hit the city. I'm sure she'll come back, though, just as she did last time."

"Insolent slave. She'll be getting more than a day locked in her room this time." Another low growl, and then the sound of a chair scraping across the floor. "Had no one seen her in Baltimore?"

Another hesitation, brief this time. "Not today, though someone mentioned that when she went with Eunice for supplies on Monday, she spent an inordinate amount of time with…"

"With? With *who*?" A creak, as if Newel leaned onto something. "A man? If she has merely taken up with someone in the city, I daresay we have nothing to worry about."

"Nay. A girl named Freeda, about her own age. Daughter of Henry Payne, the pilot."

Jack barely kept his breath from hissing out. He looked to Father, who inclined his head toward Edward. When Jack looked to his friend, the boy nodded.

What exactly did that mean? Did Freeda have something to do with the disappearance of this slave? Was that perchance what had led them here?

"A free black, then. A blight to every slave-holder in the South, those seditious rabble-rousers. They ought to be sent back to Africa, every one of them. Did you speak with her?"

Joshua loosed a laugh that sounded incredulous through the glass. "I tried, but you surely know the Paynes claim residence at the home of Thaddeus Lane. And I couldn't think you wanted me barging in there demanding answers."

"No. It wouldn't do to make an enemy of a man with so many friends. But if she was in the markets before, this girl, she will be there again. Have someone watch the stores for her and find a time to question her. Magnolia *will* be returned to me." The sound of palm slapping wood rang out. "Did you read this latest drivel in the paper?"

"By that fellow Darian? Yes, I did. A rather clever piece of satire."

"Don't tell me you've been drawn in. It is abolitionist nonsense."

"I said 'clever,' Father, not correct. Why can you never be amused by those you disagree with?"

Newel made a frustrated sound. "Go back to your books, Joshua. I have a guest due any moment."

"Yes, sir. Good evening."

"A curious guest, at that." Thad's whisper was so low Jack barely caught it. Especially as the sound of carriage wheels crunching over gravel invaded the quiet of the night. Here at the side of the house and crouched low against the wall, he couldn't see who climbed from the vehicle, but his mind certainly wasn't idle as he waited.

What had Freeda to do with all of this? That she would spend "an inordinate amount of time" talking to a slave was no great surprise—ever since she learned as a child that her mother had been born a slave, the illegitimate daughter of her former master, Freeda had taken the utmost interest in the plight of her brethren. A plight with which all their families commiserated. But if she had anything to do with the girl going missing…

No, she had more sense than that. Aiding a runaway could bring the law down on all of them. And yet—who had she been with in the cellar? He had assumed a man, and the thought of Lenna covering for their tryst hadn't set well at all. But could it have been this fugitive?

Quite possibly. Which at once eased one concern and lit to blazing a greater one. Perhaps morally this was the nobler secret, but surely the girls realized what kind of trouble they could bring upon the entire family with such actions, not to mention themselves.

His Lenna could be arrested if she were caught aiding in such schemes. Had they considered that? Not that he would let that happen. If anyone actually tried to lock up the ray of sunshine that was Julienne Lane, he would…he would do whatever it took to stop them. Anything to keep her safe.

He squeezed his eyes shut against the misty night. Why hadn't she simply told him instead of trying to keep him from the cellar? When he had seen her with mysteries in her eyes earlier today, he hadn't known what to think. They had never had secrets between them, never.

Well, no, that wasn't fair. She had never withheld secrets from him, but he kept plenty from her. Things he couldn't share because they concerned the navy. Those he knew she was happy not to know.

But what of the Culpers? Should he have told her of his involvement with her family's heritage of espionage—a heritage Thad had said she knew nothing about?

Perhaps, perhaps not. But apparently he shouldn't have entertained the question in front of her, given how she interpreted the look that must have been in his eyes. His blood heated again now at her accusation.

Father nudged his shoulder and nodded toward the window, pulling Jack's mind back to the present. The sound of an opening door came again. "Mr. Lawrence is here, suh."

"Ah." A brief pause, presumably as the guest entered, and then an exuberant, "Good evening! So glad you would deign to pay me a visit again, King Richard."

King Richard? Jack arched a brow at Father and Thad, though a shrug was his only answer.

"Good evening, Mr. Newel." The voice of *King Richard*—Lawrence, whoever he was—sounded faint and uncertain through the glass. "Kind of you to send your carriage for me again. I would bring my own, but with my inheritance still being held by the government, I cannot well afford one."

"I am happy to assist you in your time of need. Come, sit,

Your Majesty. Please. Warm yourself by the fire. How have you been this last week? And your family?"

Muted shuffling sounds followed. "I have been watching him, as you suggested. Watching his movements. And it isn't my fault, that incident with my sister. She was mocking me. I know she was."

Jack shifted, knowing his brows were knit just like Father's were. This Lawrence fellow obviously suffered from some mental malady…so why was Newel encouraging him in it?

"I am so sorry to hear of your sister's disrespect. But I daresay once you get the money you are owed by the United States and you are returned to your rightful throne, she will fall into line."

"Yes. Yes, of course. Of course she will. If only they will pay me. It is Jackson's fault, you know. Jackson's fault. If he hadn't dissolved the national bank, I would have my money."

The sound of glass clinking on glass came through the window. "Yes, I know." Newel's voice, while still filled with sympathy, carried an undertone of impatience. "The president is a bane to us all."

"It's that Jackson, that's who. We need a bank. Don't you think we need a bank? If we had a bank, they could pay me. Make me king. I'm a king."

"Hmm." A moment of silence was followed by the *thunk* of glass on table. "You say you have been observing the president's comings and goings?"

Something in Jack's stomach went tight. The same something, he would guess, that made Thad's hand clench into a fist, made Father draw in a slow breath, and made Edward shake his head.

"If he were gone, everything would be all right. Van Buren

would bring the bank back. He would give me my money. Van Buren should be president, and then everything would be all right."

Oh, Lord, what is he saying? What should we do? Jack's eyes slid shut. The ravings of a madman, nothing more...but the fact that said madman was raving *here*, in Newel's home, made unease claw at his spine.

"How right you are. President Jackson is without question the root of your problem. And as I suggested last time, I will be honored to act as your protector, King Richard, should you find a way to rid yourself of him. A king has every right to dispatch of an enemy leader, after all. It is a matter of your throne. If you do so, I will fund your trip back to England and see that your money is restored to you."

Jack opened his eyes again, though the moon glowing through the fog shrouded any answers that the world could offer. The night could not explain why a prominent planter was plotting assassination with a lunatic.

"Maybe I will. Maybe I'll do it. Tomorrow he'll be at the Capitol, at the funeral. Maybe I'll do it then. Maybe I will."

"A fine plan." Did his guest hear the overeagerness in Newel's voice? Or perhaps it couldn't penetrate whatever cloud obscured his logic. "Indeed you should. Your shop is near there. You can easily make your way to the Capitol and lie in wait. Try to get to him before the congressman's funeral. That way if you miss your chance, you will still have another opportunity on his way out."

"Yes. Yes, perhaps I'll do it."

"Perhaps? You *must*, Your Majesty. It is the only way to regain your throne. So long as Jackson is holding your money in his grip, you will remain a nobody."

"Yes, you're right. Tomorrow, then. I will act tomorrow."

Thad eased away from the house, motioning the rest of them to follow once more. Jack happily obeyed. The sooner they were away from this place and back to somewhere they could talk, the sooner he could get a few much-needed answers.

The men held their silence, though, as they crept back across the lawn, past the shack with its mournful singer. Back, finally, into the protective line of trees in which their horses waited. He swung up into his saddle as his companions did likewise.

The Newel plantation sat in the Maryland countryside, halfway between Baltimore and Washington City. On their way here, he had let himself appreciate the scenery, the beauty of the land not set about on all sides by walls. Much like his father and Thad, whom he had called uncle until recently, he preferred open spaces—especially frolicking waves. Yet Baltimore had always been home. Perhaps someday, he had thought as they arrived, he would purchase land somewhere outside the city, like Newel had done.

Just now, he wanted to have nothing in common with the man. The house Jack had purchased in Baltimore some ten months ago, in which he had spent only one night before he shipped out again, would be home enough. So long as Lenna was in it, he would need nothing else.

The claws in his spine dug deeper.

Edward reined his horse into position beside Jack's. "Do you think they'll really—"

"Let's wait to discuss it. We are still on his land." Thad glanced over his shoulder toward the big house, and then he locked gazes with Jack's father. The two had been friends so long—ever since the Arnauds escaped the Revolution in France and settled near the Lanes in Connecticut—that they probably could read each other's minds.

Jack and Lenna had always been like that too, ever since he was a child of five and introduced to Thad and Gwyn's newborn babe. He had instantly dubbed her "Lenna" rather than Julienne and had sworn from before she could speak that he always knew what she wanted. Up until today, he had believed it.

Their horses followed the path back to the foggy road, and Father glanced over at him with a lifted brow. "Now perhaps you could explain why you and Julienne scarcely spoke to each other over dinner."

Apparently Father could read Jack's mind as easily as he could Thad's. "It's nothing." He hoped. "Just a little quarrel."

Thad all but turned around in his saddle to stare. "You and Julie never quarrel."

"Which is baffling," Father added. "Jacques never hesitates to quarrel with me."

Edward snorted. "Nor does Julie with me and Win."

Jack sighed and adjusted his overcoat. It felt strange to be out of uniform. "It's nothing." It was everything.

Thad's stare hardened into a frown. "You didn't try to postpone the wedding again, did you?"

"No, he wouldn't. He isn't so big an idiot." Father added his scowl to the mix. "Are you?"

Another sigh did nothing to release the pressure building inside. "I have never suffered such a harrowing trip. I need a few days to recuperate."

Thad's frown now pronounced him as mad as the man they had just overheard. "And you would rather do it in your father's house than in your own, in the company of your bride?"

Well, when he put it like *that*… "No. But…I am so worn."

"And postponing has become a habit—a bad one." Father held his reins with one hand and rearranged his collar with the other.

"Thank you for that insight." Jack pulled his hat lower, though the fog still found a way to creep in and chill his ears and neck. "She accused me of being unfaithful."

That silenced his companions, at least until Edward snorted. "Of any other man away so long at sea, I might wonder the same. But you? She must have been riled already to even consider such a thing."

"I imagine her head knows you are a man of too much faith to betray her trust that way. But her heart…" Thad looked at him over his shoulder, his eyes looking hard as flint in the fog-wrapped moonlight. "There has been some talk lately about whether you will ever actually wed. Nothing that seems to bother her most days, but if you suggested another postponement, no matter how brief, it would have made those insecurities rear up."

"And you have known each other so long, you've no doubt forgotten to woo her." Father was apparently now an expert on wooing, though from where Jack had sat it had been Adèle doing the convincing a year ago. He sent Jack a smirk. "How long has it been since you told her how beautiful she is?"

"I say it all the time when I am home." Jack scanned the countryside for some sign of the familiar. He saw nothing, though Thad was turning them off the main road onto a rutted lane.

"Perhaps, then, you have said it too much and it has lost meaning."

A breath of laughter puffed out. "So you are saying I cannot win." But really, Father had a point. She *was* beautiful—he knew it, everyone said so. But her face was more familiar to him than his own. He had studied it so long, so intently, that it had ceased being an overall composition and had become in his mind simply *her*. His Lenna. The paradigm, the woman against whom he measured all others—and to whom no one else could ever measure up. Not because of the beauty he had long ago ceased to note, but because of the heart that always shone so brilliantly from her eyes.

"Still." Edward guided his mount a bit closer to Jack's. "She knows you too well to think you gave in to the passing charms of the entertainment your friends no doubt purchased when in foreign ports. Why would she accuse you of such a thing?"

His shoulders wanted to hunch, his tongue to defend himself against what sounded like a seed of doubt in his young friend's voice too. Instead, he sighed and looked to the elder men. "We were discussing the keeping of secrets, and this one of ours sprang to mind. She must have seen there was *something* I was holding back from her...should I have told her?"

"No!" Thad reined in his horse and sent the beast into a turn, ending up facing Jack, so close they could reach out and clasp wrists. "Are you mad?"

From any other man, the quick objection would have made Jack take offense on Lenna's behalf. Would have made him accuse the fellow of failing to see the strength behind a woman's femininity—but Thad's mother had been the original Culper in their families. Thad Lane knew, if anyone did, what a woman could accomplish in the world of the covert.

No, his objection was not to the general idea of his daughter being involved. It must be specific to Lenna. Which still made Jack frown. "I didn't. But why not?"

Thad sighed and shook his head. "You know well why not. Keeping such secrets would tie Julie in knots. It isn't her nature. She is all openness and sunshine."

That she was. And her father was right. Which was why her behavior that afternoon had been so very strange. "What am I to tell her, then? How am I to assure her I'm not about illicit business when I'm seeing to Culper affairs? Gwyn knows what you do, Thad, and that your parents were in it together too. How can I carry this mantle and yet keep it from her?"

"I wish I had an answer to that." Casting his gaze out into the night, he shook his head again. "All I can tell you is every time I considered educating my daughter about this, I distinctly felt I should not. Perhaps because she would not handle it well. Perhaps because she has a cause of her own now that demands her attention."

Invisible waves lapped at Jack, threatening to swallow him whole. "Please tell me Lenna and Freeda are not aiding runaways. Please, please tell me I misread that bit we overheard back there."

Edward had come to a halt on Jack's other side. "It's mostly Freeda. Julie has been too busy penning articles that have the entire South in an uproar."

Those articles... "The ones the Newels were discussing?" By the mysterious "Darian"—Greek for "freedom." Jack's eyes slid shut. He had only read one of them in one of the few papers they had gotten their hands on during their time at sea. And for every sailor who agreed with the cleverly disguised abolitionist sentiments, another had cursed the writer and declared him— her?—an anarchist.

"One and the same." Pride rang in Thad's voice. "Though the girls don't realize we know, either about the runaways or the writing. And we let them think it, as the less either is discussed, the safer for them both."

Of course. That was what Lenna had wanted to show him, to tell him—her writing. But Freeda's secret she would not be so quick to share with him.

He should have let it drop.

"Come." Thad wheeled his horse around again. "There is a cabin around this bend where we can light a fire and discuss it all."

The thought of a warm fire spurred them all on at a quick pace, but Jack's thoughts raced even faster. At least Thad and Edward were aware of what Freeda was doing. That meant they were watching, however invisibly, and ensuring the safety of the girls.

But still. The thought of spitfire Freeda or sunny Lenna being locked up and possibly even executed…he whispered a wordless prayer, a soul-deep plea.

"The wedding is still on as planned, though, isn't it?" Edward's scowl combined curiosity with concern. "Neither of you said anything at dinner about postponing it. And if you were to do so, you must let everyone know now—there are hordes of people coming from Washington City and Annapolis, and all the family has already arrived from Connecticut."

Only by force did he keep his hands from tightening around the reins. Of course they hadn't enough time to postpone—ironic, given that it was the lack of time that made him wish for just a day or two more to rest before the hordes descended. But Thad was right that he would better enjoy the relaxation when doing it at his own house, with his bride by his side. According to dinner conversation, Lenna and her mother and Adèle had been making trips to the new house at least once a week, seeing to its furnishings and decorations. By now it was no doubt more her home than his.

But now there was *this*, this nebulous chasm between them. The secrets they couldn't share, or hadn't. The sudden and awkward realization of them, the questions they could never unspeak. The fact that he hadn't let things drop and trusted her when she asked him to.

And then she had questioned the two things he held most dear—his faith and his promise.

What was a man without those? How could she accuse him of unfaithfulness and then, in her next breath, belittle the importance of his word?

He had given that word when he was a boy of nine, when four-year-old Lenna had looked up at him with those big blue eyes of hers and asked, "Can I marry you someday, Jacky?"

Maybe most men would forget such silly childhood promises, but he hadn't. He had meant it then, when he had taken her chubby hand in his and promised to stay beside her for the rest of their lives—and he meant it no less now. They were knit together like a tapestry. He couldn't even entertain the question of *if* they would work through this.

They must. That was the only option.

"Well?"

He nearly jumped at Edward's quiet voice, barely remembering where his thoughts had begun—with the young man's question about the wedding. He summoned up a smile as Thad and Father drew to a halt outside a ramshackle building nestled between the trees. "There is no need to fret, Ed. Lenna and I will figure this out."

"Well, you had better be quick about it. You have only tomorrow to do your figuring."

"And tomorrow seems to be a day of trouble." After wrapping his horse's reins around a wobbly post, Thad opened the door. "What are we to do about this bizarre assassination plan, gentlemen?"

The silence cracked as they all walked inside. It grew while Father set about lighting the tinder already laid in the old Franklin stove. And when Thad lit a lamp, the silence solidified.

They must all be thinking the same thing. Andrew Jackson wasn't a man any one of them liked. He stood for everything they stood against. He put down all they fought for. He treated with disdain those they embraced as equals.

But he was still the president. And with the title came the respect. More, he was a man—and no man deserved to be plotted against, even if he wasn't above plotting the destruction of others.

Father loosed a gusty, very French sigh and slouched into a rickety chair. "I suppose we cannot let the poor lunatic go through with it. He cannot possibly know what he is doing. Did you ask about him today, Thad?"

"Hmm. Under the guise of looking for a house painter, which is his profession." Thad leaned into the wall beside the stove. "Apparently, a few months ago the man had some kind of mental break. His family is all quite worried, especially as he becomes belligerent and violent with no provocation."

Perfect prey for someone like Newel then. He had perhaps found the man just as Thad had. Although…Jack looked from one companion to another. "How did you even learn of this?"

Edward jerked his head toward Baltimore. "The slave that ran away. I overheard her and Freeda yesterday in the cellar, and she said something about how scared she was her master was going to get them all in trouble. She said enough that I started wondering."

"You were right to do so." Thad rubbed a hand over his face. "It would be so easy to do nothing. Yet we all know the Lord led that girl to our home for a reason. The Lord means us to act."

"Then act we must." Jack stretched his hands out toward the stove and watched the flicker of orange flame. "There is a funeral tomorrow?"

Father nodded. "At the Capitol, yes. We were planning to attend anyway."

"Alain and I can join the crowd as planned and work to keep the president always surrounded by the masses," said Thad. "I daresay that is all it will take to dissuade Lawrence."

Perhaps...but Jack shook his head. "We oughtn't to risk it. We should work from his end too. Go to his home or shop beforehand and take his weapons—"

"How would we find them? Or know how many he has?" Edward looked to the ceiling. "I think we would do better to wait until he is out, when he cannot fetch anything but what he has on his person. *Then* take them."

"Take a man's pistols in public, and one risks him crying 'thief' and bringing undo attention upon us." Father tapped a hand against his trousers. "But you have the right idea, boys. You must make sure he cannot take a shot even if the president is unguarded."

"Take a shot." Jack's gaze went unfocused as his mind clicked through it all. "If there is any lesson I learned at sea, it is that the enemy of a shot, be it in canon or pistol or rifle, is water. If we can but slip a few drops into his powder supply, it would render it all useless, no matter what weapon he tried to fire."

"We can handle that." With a smile a little too eager, Edward slapped Jack in the arm. "Right, Jack?"

"We can. But stopping Lawrence doesn't stop Newel, does it? Why is he involved in this?" Jack sent his gaze toward Thad, figuring if anyone knew...

But his soon-to-be father-in-law shook his head. "I cannot say. I know Newel has had some fiscal setbacks that coincided with Jackson's closing of the national bank. Perhaps they are related. Perhaps he blames the president for them just as 'King Richard' does."

Edward shifted closer to the fire. "The girl said something about him almost getting found out along with Randolph a year ago. Anyone know what she meant?"

At that, Jack snapped upright. "Robert Randolph? He was a naval officer caught embezzling. When he was discovered, Jackson dismissed him. Randolph tried to club him with a cane not long after. It was all the men could talk of for weeks at sea."

"Well, then." Thad's grin matched his son's. "If he was involved in that, I will find the proof of it easily enough and make it quite clear to Mr. Newel that if anything happens to the president, knowledge about his deeds will be made quite public. Perhaps even at the hands of our rather eloquent Darian."

How could both pride and longing, both anticipation and exhaustion seep through him at the thought of all his Lenna had done in his absence and he had to do on the morrow? Save a president, blackmail a villain—and somehow convince the only woman he had ever wanted that his promise meant more now than ever.

Three

Never in her life had Lenna trudged through a morning with so much despair. She sat in the icy carriage beside her grandmother and put her feet by rote on the hot brick beneath her, but she felt neither the cold nor heat. To be sure, life had buzzed on as usual around her all morning. Her family had chatted and laughed as always, Freeda had liberated some food from the kitchen for her fugitive, more wedding gifts had arrived.

But hollowness echoed within her as she visualized the boxes and packages in the parlor along with the other items that needed to be taken to what would be—*should* be, *might* be— her home tomorrow. Why had she agreed to the impromptu trip into Washington City for last-minute shopping while the menfolk attended a funeral? She was poor company indeed.

Squeezing her eyes shut tight, she scarcely held back her tears as the carriage rumbled to a halt. Jack had said nothing last night to their parents to indicate the wedding wouldn't take place.

But then, he had said nothing to her to make her think it would. He had said nothing to her at all.

She shouldn't have asked such a thing of him yesterday. The hurt that had flashed through his eyes… Well, if she really wondered, that was all the answer she needed. She knew Jack too well, knew he would never betray her trust. Knew she meant too much to him, and more, knew his faith in the Lord would never permit it.

Why had she given voice to such an awful doubt? She was horrible. She didn't deserve for Jack to forgive her, to love her, to marry her. There he was, serving their nation, climbing the ranks of the navy, being daily the sort of hero other men could only hope to someday be, and she greeted him with accusation and distrust.

"Julie." Her mother caught her by the hand, drawing her attention from her roiling thoughts and back to the crowded streets around them. She scarcely remembered climbing from the carriage, but now she couldn't even spot Papa with them. He must have met up already with Alain. And Jack? "What is wrong? You have been in another world today, and it doesn't look to be a happy one."

A deep breath helped her focus, though it failed to fill the emptiness inside. Still, she summoned a smile for her mother and sent it to Grandmama Winter too, where that lady stood with a matching crease of concern to her brow. "Call it wedding nerves, I suppose."

Mama gave her fingers a squeeze. "You both acted so strangely at dinner last night. Did something happen?"

Everything. Nothing. She sighed. "We argued. Which we have not done since we were children, not really, and now…"

"Ah." Grandmama took her other hand, confidence

gleaming in her emerald eyes. "The solution is obvious then." She nodded across the street, to the open area before the Capitol.

To where Jack and Edward slid through a gathering crowd.

"Go make amends, sweet one, before any more time is wasted on tears when you should be smiling."

Could it be so simple? Could the gap be bridged just by running to him now as she hadn't done yesterday?

As she watched his distant figure, he turned. Not looking at her—he wouldn't even realize she was in the city, given that the women's decision to come had been made at the last moment—but still. Glimpsing his smile as he exchanged a word with her brother was enough to remind her of why her heart had always been bound to his. There was no man in the world like her Jack.

"Mama?"

Her mother chuckled and released her hand. "Go put things to rights and enjoy an hour about the town with Jack. Just meet us at the milliner's by one o'clock."

Lenna's smile felt more like itself as she sped away from them, down the street toward her love. So far as she knew, he and Edward were not planning to attend the funeral, but perhaps they wanted to speak with someone beforehand. They certainly seemed to be scouring the crowds. Not for their fathers, apparently, because they looked right past them—and there was no missing Papa's height.

Apparently they found who they sought. They split up and approached a man from two sides, Edward from in front and Jack behind.

Odd. Edward made a too-effusive greeting, his demeanor more Papa's than his own. And while he fawned—there was no other word for it—over the fellow, Jack moved cautiously behind him.

What was that he was doing, reaching toward the man? Had she not known better, she would have thought him a pickpocket. But no, if Jack were taking something from someone, it would be for the best of reasons.

Frowning, Lenna sidestepped a puddle and held her cape closed against a blast of cold, damp wind. The fellow seemed to sense something was amiss, but Edward got his attention again, and even earned what looked like a laugh. Jack made a few more small moves, and then he eased away, nodding at her brother. A moment later, Edward made a courtly bow and took his leave too.

Odd indeed. But even as she wondered what in the world they had just done, she saw Edward make a sign toward Papa, who watched them from a fair distance. If she made out the gesture correctly, he said simply *Done*.

Something Papa had tasked them with, then. Which may not have dimmed her curiosity, but it made her lips turn up. Papa and Alain—and more recently Edward—had no idea she knew they snuck out at all hours on some covert business about which they never spoke in her presence. And while she didn't know *what* they were doing, she didn't have to. It was enough to know they were doing it, and doing good in the process.

Her eyes tracked back to Jack. He must be part of the same business, whatever it was. Which she ought to have guessed.

Oh! *That* secret was surely what she had seen in his eyes yesterday! Foolish man, why didn't he just say his secrets were tied to her father's? Surely he knew that was all she required to be satisfied. When she caught up with him, she would toss her arms around him, never mind the audience, and tell him just that.

Her gaze still on Jack, she didn't notice the closer figure until a gentleman stepped directly into her path. Large and dressed to intimidate in a fur-trimmed overcoat and tall top hat over his silver hair, the man came to a halt. Squealing in alarm, she barely pulled up in time to keep from plowing directly into him.

"Oh, excuse me." Dash it, why did the man just stand there, glowering at her and taking up the entire sidewalk? She tried to step around him, but he moved to block her path. "Pardon me, sir."

The man narrowed his eyes to two slits. Rather beady ones, at that, what with a foul temper making them gleam, though if he smiled he might be quite handsome. "I know who you are."

Five little words, yet they made her mouth go dry, her throat contract. Impossible. She had never met this man before. He couldn't possibly know she was John Darian, essayist. Even the editors who published her work knew not who sent it; she was always very careful. The most any of them knew was that Darian hailed from Baltimore.

No, he couldn't know. Not that. So she straightened to her full height, remembered the poise her mother—descended of English and French nobility both—had instilled, and lifted her chin. "Then you have me at a disadvantage, sir, for I have no idea who you may be."

He didn't seem inclined to make introductions. He slid half a step closer, leaning in far too much for courtesy. "You are Thad Lane's daughter, and the friend of that upstart Negress."

Freeda! What have you done now? Or perhaps it was something she had done before—hard to say when one had helped at least half a dozen slaves escape north over the last two years. Lenna lifted a brow. "Congratulations, sir. You know what all of Maryland does."

The fur trim on his overcoat seemed to bristle when his shoulders bunched. "You listen to me, Miss Lane." He lifted his cane to punctuate, his mustache twitching. "And you tell that wench to listen too. I'll have my property back if I have to hunt her down all the way into Canada."

Lenna blinked. "Oh, you poor man. Have you lost your dog?"

A vein strained for freedom in his neck. "A slave, as you well know. And *I* know that seditious freewoman of yours had something to do with it."

Lightning flashed in his eyes, thunder rumbled in his throat. And though heaven's fury never ceased to make anxiety knot her stomach, she would *not* be intimidated by some arrogant planter. She fastened on her sweetest smile. "I'm afraid you're mistaken, sir. Though I count a freewoman as my closest friend, she is not seditious and never seeks trouble." No, she rather hunted it down like an Amazon warrior.

Another flash of lightning, dark instead of bright. "You tell her, Miss Lane. You tell her that I'll have my recompense. That if I cannot find proof to haul her to the gallows, I'll take my vengeance some other way. She'll turn around one night and find me waiting, and she'll wish she had never set eyes on my Magnolia."

A gust of icy wind swept up the street, but she couldn't blame it for the shiver skittering up her spine. Never in her life had she seen such oily hatred in a man's eyes. *Giver of all, give me strength now, I pray You!*

A fingerprint of warmth touched her heart. The breath

she drew in was long instead of panicked, the step she took backward decisive.

The arm that settled around her waist blessed and familiar, as was the cinnamon scent that filled her nose. *Jack.*

"Mr. Newel, isn't it?" His baritone resonated through that empty place, filled it with a song. "Are you threatening my betrothed?"

The man straightened, eyes shifting to neutral. "Certainly not, Mr—or rather, Lieutenant."

She aimed her smile up, to the side, into the profile that set a far different skitter racing up and down her back. "He was threatening Freeda. He seems to think she might have been involved with the disappearance of one of his slaves."

Though to Mr. Newel's gaze Jack's face would only look amused, she saw the acknowledgment in the deep brown eyes he turned on her. "Our Freeda? Nonsense. A more docile, sweet-tempered young woman you could never meet."

She very nearly laughed. "That is what I was trying to tell him."

"Argue all you like. But give her my warning." Mr. Newel motioned at them with his cane. "And the two of you had better stay out of my way."

"Again you are mistaken, sir." Lenna's smile faded, her brows lifted again. "You are the one who stepped into mine."

Something about the way Jack chuckled, low and quiet in his throat, made her think he knew the thoughts running through her mind—that she would have to make it a point to discover all Mr. Newel's positions so Darian could lambast them in the press.

The man huffed a step away before Jack lifted a hand. "Oh, Mr. Newel? Next time you see Randolph, give him my regards."

Though she had no idea who Randolph was, Mr. Newel obviously did. He froze, though he didn't turn to face them again.

When she glanced up at Jack's face, she saw the same mask of command she'd chafed at yesterday. Funny how much more she liked it today.

"Tread carefully, sir," he said quietly. Somehow, the words were all the more menacing for their lack of volume. "Your associations are not unknown. One more false step, and you won't be chasing your escaped slaves to Canada. You'll be fleeing there yourself."

All she could see of Mr. Newel's reaction was the tic in his jaw. Without any other response, he strode away.

Lenna turned wide eyes on her beloved. "Now, Jack. Whatever did Canada do to deserve the likes of him?"

The mask fractured, split, and then slipped away under the force of his laugh. "Ah, Lenna. I should have known the moment I first read that article. Your wit is like no one else's."

He *did* know, which meant someone must have told him. Freeda? It had to be, unless her family had figured it out. Possible, granted. But of no consequence right now. Grinning, she clasped his hand and pulled him along the sidewalk another few steps, and then into the first alley that presented itself. "Come. I owe you something."

"Oh?"

"Indeed." Spying a handy stack of crates to serve as a blind, she tugged him into their shelter. And then leapt into his arms.

Arms that closed around her and held her tight. "Ah, yes. And I have a debt to pay too." Dipping his head under the wide front brim of her bonnet, he found her lips and seared them with his own. So warm against the January chill, so right against all the wrong, so safe amidst the storm.

Had she doubted? Impossible. There was no place to be but in his arms. No tomorrow but with him. No promise in the world but his word.

"I love you," he murmured against her lips a long minute later, holding her tight against him. "I'm so sorry for how I behaved yesterday."

"Not as sorry as I. I never should have questioned—"

"It was reasonable. But I swear to you, I would never—"

"I know." Seeing that same look in his eye again though, that same shadow pass through them, she touched a finger to his lips. "And I don't need to know. You and Edward and our fathers do whatever it is you do, and that is well and good. I needn't be a part of it."

When he kissed her fingertip, a delicious trill swept through her. And when he grinned at her like that, her knees went weak. "I suppose you have causes enough of your own, Miss...Darian."

She tightened her arms around his neck and kissed him again, quick and teasing. "I tried to tell you."

"I know. I'm sorry. I should have listened, so I could tell you how proud I am." He ran a hand up her back and feathered his lips over her jaw. "Lenna?"

How had she survived nine months without him? How would she do it again when spring came? "Hmm?"

"Will you marry me tomorrow?"

Oh, that was how. He always knew how to fill her heart enough that it could carry her through their separations. "You're sure? We could push it back a week. A week is no great trouble. You have to know I was lying when I said I would wait no longer. I'll wait forever to be yours."

"Tomorrow. I'm sure."

"You promise?" Because if he did, it would be enough. It was always enough. From her first memories, any word he spoke she knew she could trust.

He cupped her cheek and touched his lips to hers again. "I promise." And then he pulled away, eyes alight. "Walk with me?"

"Happily." Her hand tucked in the crook of his arm, she scarcely noticed the wind as they regained the street. Her steps matched to his, they could have been the only people in all of Washington City.

Winding their way through buildings nearly as familiar to her as those of her own city, she soaked it all in. Yes, she would have to issue a warning to Freeda, cautioning her friend to avoid Mr. Newel at all costs. Yes, she would have to think of her next article, of how best to rouse the masses with the biting wit Darian had become famous for.

Yes, she would have to bid farewell to her love again when the fleet took once more to the seas—and likely many more times beforehand, for a few hours here and there as he disappeared with her father.

But now, just now, she had not a care to burden her. She had her very own hero at her side, and tomorrow she would be his wife. Today, all she needed was to stroll by his side and talk of everything and nothing.

He halted them near the East Portico of the Capitol as the doors flung open and the black-clad men exited the funeral service within. Lenna watched the politicians and businessmen

file out, familiar faces and familiar names. Vice President Van
Buren, Secretary Eaton, David Crockett, and President Jackson.

Though she didn't know the man who stepped away from
the portico as the president passed. No wait…was that the
fellow Jack and Edward had found earlier?

A gasp found purchase when the man reached into his coat,
pulled out a pistol, and aimed it at the president's back. "Jack!"
Her throat too tight for it to be but a whisper, she dug her
fingers into his arm.

Jack's hand covered hers as the man pulled the trigger.

Nothing.

A vile curse ringing, he produced a second pistol, pulled
the trigger again as the crowd pulsed and recoiled.

No shot amid the shouts.

"Good heavens." She didn't know where to look—at the
president and Mr. Crockett coming at the would-be attacker
with canes and fists, or at the man at her side who stood so
calmly by.

Jack, as always, won out.

He watched the melee for a moment, and then he turned
her away.

"Jack." But what to say? What to ask? She shook her head.
"Did that man just attempt to kill the president? And did *both*
his guns misfire?"

"So it would seem, my love." He slanted a grin down at her.
"Blasted humidity, no doubt."

Hmm. "No doubt."

Ah, well. Let him keep his adventures and intrigues and
mysteries. Her words were sword enough for her.

Author's Note

On January 30, 1835, America witnessed the very first attempted assassination of its president. Andrew Jackson was a man who polarized the people. His heroics during the War of 1812 had won him his position, but the same spirit that made him a menace to the British in the war made him enemies aplenty among his own people too.

This assassination attempt still makes historians scratch their heads. Richard Lawrence was by all accounts mentally unbalanced—today, people assume it a result of lead poisoning from his house-painting business. Then, all they knew was that he suddenly went from a docile, friendly man to one prone to violent outbursts...and who fancied himself the long-dead King Richard III of England. Somehow or another he got it into his head that the only reason he wasn't on the throne of England was because the United States had stolen his inheritance, and now couldn't give it back because Jackson dissolved the national bank. After both his pistols misfired on that fateful January day (which historians assume must have been a result of damp air), he was captured by the president and Davy Crocket, tried, and found not guilty on account of insanity.

But everyone wondered, then and now, if he hatched this plot all on his own...or perhaps was put up to it. I decided that was a fine premise for my little story. I enjoyed delving into the relationship of my Jack and Lenna, and I hope you enjoyed this glimpse of their love, and will join me in *Circle of Spies* to see them as the parents of my fiery heroine. And if you haven't already, you can read more about the Lanes and Arnauds in *Whispers from the Shadows*, where Jack is but a precocious four-year-old that I hope will make you smile as much as he did me. Happy reading!

Printed in the USA
CPSIA information can be obtained
at www.ICGtesting.com
LVHW031218181023
761344LV00033B/382